# Guard

Satan's Pride Series

by

A. G. Kirkham

DORRANCE
PUBLISHING CO
EST. 1920
PITTSBURGH, PENNSYLVANIA 15235

The contents of this work, including, but not limited to, the accuracy of events, people, and places depicted; opinions expressed; permission to use previously published materials included; and any advice given or actions advocated are solely the responsibility of the author, who assumes all liability for said work and indemnifies the publisher against any claims stemming from publication of the work.

Dorrance Publishing Co
585 Alpha Drive
Suite 103
Pittsburgh, PA 15238
Visit our website at *www.dorrancebookstore.com*

ISBN: 978-1-4809-2972-2
eISBN: 978-1-4809-2351-5

# Prologue

My BMW SUV is packed with the essentials, and the gas tank is full. I'm ready for the extensive and exciting drive to the new place I'm calling home. It was a difficult decision to make but New York just didn't fill me the same way it has in the past.

Everything is different now. James has been gone for three years and the emptiness has not faded. The aching hurt from his death has subsided and I still can't find my "happy." What was once our home for five lovely years are just memories of my loss.

I am leaving Becca (short for Rebecca) and Brian Duncan, my two best friends. They found each other now and have a little Duncan on the way. I promised them I would visit when the baby is due and I always keep my promises. It's so wonderful that they finally found each other. Years of working together on set and everyone knew they had a "thing" for each other except the two of them. Brian worked behind the camera taking picture after picture of Becca whether she was posing or not. He loved her from the first. He fought it! Man, was he in denial. Brian is a photographer and has models lined up outside his studio. His smiling green eyes, broad shoulders, lean six-foot-one-inch build, and short cropped blond hair attracted the ladies. And since they came to him, he took them. His talent as a photographer made him one of the most sought after in the world. Models wanted to sleep with him and wanted their pictures taken from him. Not necessarily in that order but both came very easy to Brian.

Becca is the controlled model. She gave nothing away until the camera pointed to her. She is a five foot nine inches beauty with thick blonde hair with natural curl. She had the model look, feel and pose. She walked the catwalk proud and every dress looked desirably impressive when she put it on. Follow that up with a perky nose and full lips, you have a blonde goddess. And somehow my two friends after years of playing cat and mouse finally caught each other.

Of course, they couldn't do this without drama! Another photographer was showing great interest in Becca and then decided he wanted to pursue her romantically. That set Brian on a rampage. Our dear sweet "friend" became a lunatic! How adorably sweet! I love that this happened for them both. They have each other and I need to move on so that I can find my "happy" again.

Hands on the wheel, no looking back, turning the key in the ignition, and go!

My trip was made really easy with the GPS and the thoughts of my cottage-like home right on the lake. It was just perfect! I had the home remodeled when I first bought it six months ago and finally the renovations were complete.

It was a cozy, homey-styled home. The main floor was open concept with huge eat in kitchen because I love to cook. Deep espresso-colored cupboards, modern steel appliances, a wicked chrome sink and a granite countertop. Made for me! The main floor also has a family room, spare bedroom with its own private bath, and another powder room off the laundry area. My home was modern with a twist of warm and comforting. I created warmth and comfort with colors, patterns, soft rugs and comfy sofas and plush chairs. Let's not forget the pillows! I love pillows. They are soft and kick ass designed. The rooms were soft cocoa and pale yellows with highlights of deep burgundy and orange.

My favourite part of the house was the loft! I turned this into my master bedroom suite. It has it all a five-piece state-of-the-art bathroom with soft cream and antique blue tiles, a claw tub, and separate matching shower, sink and toilet. It has a massive walk in closet. After all I am a girl and a girl need to have a place for wardrobe and killer heels. Most of all I loved the floor-to-ceiling windows and terrace. I can see the lake from my window and sit out on the terrace and just breathe.

My life is changing and although I am taking pieces of my old life with me I am creating something new. I am going to teach dance in my new studio adjacent to my cottage haven.

Of course I am no fool! I know that I will still model because I am still in demand for specific looks and trends. I am not the typical model! I started off as a dancer and have been dancing since I was four years old. I began in ballet, then modern and added ballroom to my repertoire. I think my favourite is freestyle. This is where I let the music flow through me and I just move as I feel. I love to dance and I love to choreograph. Somehow my dancing and unique look opened the door for me to accept some modeling gigs and they liked me enough to keep calling me back. Bonus!

Somewhat insane actually, as I am five foot seven, long deep silky chestnut hair, defined nose, full lips and high cheekbones and I think I have pretty green eyes. At least, this is what I am told. I am also told that that whenever I pose for the photographers, just the "right look" is created. Of course, I have no idea if this is true and I know the lifespan of my field. I am lucky to be modeling at my age. I am thirty-five! That's old for my industry! But as long as I get some calls and I get say in what I wear and how I pose, then I will continue.

Four hours later and I was entering the town of Bournham just outside of Boston, Massachusetts. Turning into town I decided to pick up groceries. I need to eat and I might as well do it now. I quickly parked my car headed into the Local Grocer market. As I got closer to the front doors of the market I noticed ten to twelve motorcycles. Alongside those bikes I saw some massive men. Tall, big and looking a little menacing. I am assuming the women with them were their biker babes. They were smiling and laughing. Arms around their men and looking very possessive, all while touching them. Looks like they found their "happy." I am not ashamed to admit that a little pang of envy hit me right then.

Get over it! Move on! Get in, shop and get out!

I hop out of my car, smoothing over my snug Capri jeans that I matched with a cute capped sleeve deep green t-shirt. I finished this off with simple strappy cream sandals with green rhinestone decorating the heels. I decided that the best way to not be intimidated by big bad biker dudes it to pretend they don't exist. So I keep moving right past the gaggle of Satan's Pride MC jackets and their ladies and bikes, with a little sigh of relief when I get in the door. I could feel eyes following me as I walked past them and through the main doors.

Ignore it! Just ignore it! God, let them be gone when I leave!

# Chapter 1
# Close Encounter

My cart was full. I took my time to pick up everything I was going to need for the first week of life in Bournham. All the staples and then some! I was a healthy eater and despite the life of models I refused to fall prey to the starvation tactics to stay in an industry that would eventually have no place for me. I had curves and I was in demand because these curves fit the ads and designers that want women to wear their clothes, not waifs with sullen sadness haunting their faces.

I had a nice chat with Molly. Apparently she was the owner's wife. A pretty woman in her mid-forties with a halo of sandy-coloured curls and fuller hourglass curves. Molly was certainly friendly and babbled on with gusto. In a very short time I knew that the main street hosted a variety of businesses. The diner had the best coffee and I need to make time to go visit Milly and Benny the owners and also her sister and brother-in-law. The bakery made fresh scones every Sunday and supplied the church with cookies for coffee time after 9 A.M. mass. The drycleaner was always late opening; the hardware store was open even if the sign says closed because Mr. Becker couldn't remember to switch it every day. I learned quite a bit! We shared some "nothing" chatter and although I could see that she was fishing for information I kept my chatting to pleasantries. I did make very sure that I smiled sweetly and thanked her for taking the time to say hello and welcome me.

Crap! Half-hour later and they were still out there. I was paying for my groceries and I can still see the sea of motorcycles and Satan's Pride jackets.

"Miss," called the young lady at the till. Her nametag said Alice. She looked to be late thirties with a sweet knowing smile. Alice had caught on that I am feeling a little insecure about walking back out into the parking lot with the rowdy group bikers hanging about.

"Yes," I replied. My eyes moving towards hers and I deliberately soften my face to release the sternness in my brows.

"Would you like some help getting those groceries into your car?" she asked, giving me a small wink and brought a slight smile to my lips and my eyes lit up.

"I would appreciate it," I said calmly, hoping that I did not share my anxiety of walking past the Satan's Pride outside. I gave a grateful smile and Alice called Eddie to assist me with my bags.

As luck would have it, Eddie walked with me to my car and helped me load it all. Such a lovely older man in his sixties who is working at the market to fill some time during his day until his wife Dianne decides to retire from teaching and then they could travel together. In ten short minutes Eddie shared his love for his five grandchildren and fishing for trout. Eddie had lived here all his life and told me that this was the best place ever to be and even with his desire to travel he was always coming home. I was glad to hear that because I was here to stay.

Mainly, I was happy to have been able to concentrate on Eddie and make it past the market doors to my car. I thanked Eddie and promised I would be back sometime next week to fill up again. The banter from the group of Satan's Pride sounded a lot like teasing but the loudness and gruffness made it sound more like they were about to do battle with one another. I sat in my car for a few minutes thrilled that I decided that my deep blue SUV needed tinted windows when I bought it and it served me well today. I am safe in my car, doors locked; so why am I feeling vulnerable?

Why am I feeling watched? I am sure they didn't even notice me and I am behaving like a nut. Good heavens, I am from New York! The land of muggers and I am worried about a few bikes outside a market. "Get a grip, Ava Talbot!" I told myself. I must be tired and just out of sorts. The last few days have been a blur and I must be over sensitive.

I turn on the car and back out of my parking space. I am leaving the lot when I notice one of the big bad biker dudes staring at me (or rather my car, 'cause I have tinted windows so I am safe, right?). What is he staring at? Those steel-blue eyes are directed right at me. What the hell?!

He must be six feet four! And muscle! And more muscle! He is huge and chiselled. He looks like a ripped heavyweight fighter with steel blue eyes and dark wavy hair that covered his forehead and a sexy goatee. I snap my brain back into drive. I have no idea how I managed to pull my shit together but I was out of the lot and on my way home. Wait! Did I just say sexy goatee?

It was another ten minutes but I was finally in my Shangri-La. It was beautiful. And peaceful. I hit the garage door opener, and drive in. I am home.

After unpacking the groceries, unpacking the car, making up my bed, and making a simple omelet for dinner, I was too exhausted to think of anything else. I locked up the house and headed to up to my deliciously enticing bed. Not thirty seconds after laying my head on my pillow, I must have dropped off.

Since I had no place to be I played lazy gal the next morning. I lounged on my terrace overlooking my lake sipping my coffee. I pulled out my notebook and decided to officially launch my dance studio. I am going to concentrate on kid's enrollment first. I taught all through school so I had the means, ability and credentials to teach dance. I researched the town before I purchased my home and property and they expressed an interest in having recreational programs for the kids in the town.

I put my best laid plans on paper and began sending off emailed to the mayor, the schools and the churches in the area to make them aware of the classes I was offering. I also expanded that I also teach adults however would be tailoring to the needs of the individual instead of classes for the time being.

After twenty-two emails and four cups of coffee, I was ready for a shower and a late breakfast of poached eggs on toast. After my shower I was going to head down to the lake. I am going to sit on my dock and have my toes touch the water as I read. I love to read, almost as much as I love to dance and music. Of course I see dance and music connected. The music moves my soul to fly through dance.

Wearing my cutoff jean shorts and ribbed blue tank top with flip-flops on my feet, I head to my dock. With my book in one hand and a cold water bottle in the other, I walk down and plop myself at the edge of the dock. Toes dangling and my mind free to imagine the words on the pages I am reading. Peaceful!

It's been two seeks since leaving New York and with nightly calls from Becca that sounded like a looped recording.

"Come home," Becca insists.

"Becca, I am home. I like it here. I need to be here at least for now," I respond calmly.

"This is crazy and you are just running away! In the two weeks you have been there you still cannot tell me anything about the people in that town. You are hibernating! You need to talk and be around people," she continues.

"I'm actually on my way into town this morning," I say sweetly. I give her a quick kiss over the phone and a short "Bye." That was a little fib. And now I am uncomfortable with this lie so I now need to go into town.

DAMN! I have been back to town for groceries but I haven't ventured out to explore yet.

You catch the drift right. I hate lying and being lied to. So I am going to town. I pull on my jeans and simple white peasant blouse that hangs loose and I cinch that with a deep brown thick belt that tightens the material giving it the simple yet chic appearance. I want to look nice but not make it seem like I am trying too hard to fit in. I pair the outfit with my pretty slip on ballet sandals and take a wrist purse instead of full purse. I only need to fit keys, gloss and cash and a driver's license. Hair in tight ponytail, small diamond studs and makeup free except a little gloss on my lips and I am ready to go.

I walk through the town and take in all the main stores. One side of the main strip is small shops, anything from vintage clothing to a law office. The other side has a tattoo place, mechanic's shop, auto and bike parts store and some other retail stores. The mechanic's shop had the Satan's Pride MC group standing in a huddle. They all seemed pretty intense in their conversation. It is unfortunate but I need to walk past the shop in order to get to my destination of the greatest coffee (according to Molly from the market). The diner was right in view. I needed coffee. I take a deep breath and make my legs move forward.

I keep my eyes on the prize. I keep my eyes forward on the diner. I am from New York and we are the best at indifference. Unfortunately, I don't think the Satan's Pride crew knew that I was from New York. I can hear the whistles and catcalls. Of course at this point I am right in front of the shop and I if I turned my head even slightly I would have a full view of the entire crew.

# Guard

I almost reacted! AND I do mean almost! I stopped myself quick enough to continue at the same pace. I did not quicken my pace; turn my head or flinch, not even a little bit. That is until I heard a growl from the crowd of bikers.

"Ignoring us doesn't mean we don't exist, sweetness."

I didn't even have to look to know that this came from their leader. I also knew that if I turned my head I was going to confront those steely blue eyes. I am not a coward. I will not be intimidated. I take a deep breath and turn my head and sure enough I meet those eyes. I purposely redirect my steps towards the shop and to the warrior that stands arms crossed in a "know-it-all" stance.

I move standing three feet from the rock-hard-body-and-sexy-as-hell biker. I pull off my sunglasses and look right into his eyes. The stare down continues for what seems an eternity. Then I broke the silence.

"I believe you were saying," I said, tilting my head a tad.

"We live here, sweetness. We aren't going anywhere and you walking past us pretending not to notice us doesn't mean we don't see you," he said.

I could see the glint in his eyes. He thinks I am going to fall apart. He is waiting for me to run.

"I didn't realize my acknowledgement of you existing meant so much to you," I said quietly. I then scanned the rest of the faces and smiled sweetly and continued, "Good morning, gentlemen. Have a great start to your day." I then turned back to leader warrior biker dude. "I trust we're good now?" I asked.

Well, the group erupted in laughter, except warrior man.

"Well, she isn't going to run, Guard! Girl has attitude! Good choice, man!" exclaimed the man next to him, smacking Guard on the back of the shoulder. He was a couple of inches shorter to the man they called Guard. He had sun-kissed blond hair that reached the base of his thick neck. Although they both had blue eyes, this burly man had a lighter shade of blue.

What the hell did he mean, he made a good choice? What choice? Whatever! Not my problem.

The confusion must have shown across my face and my eyes went back to Guard. What the hell kind of a name was Guard anyway? I stood my ground for what seemed eons and when I was just about ready to back away and turn my attention back to the diner, steely-blue-eyed Guard took a step closer to me.

Shit!

Three feet turning to two feet and two feet became a few inches away from me. At this point I had to crank my neck upward and he was hovering over me.

It took all my resolve to stand my ground. He looked every bit the giant next to me. His frame was the size of a football player. His arms are massive and although he had uncrossed them he looked no less menacing. His lips curled into a very sly smile and he bent down so that his lips were next to my ear.

"You belong to me. Every part of your delectable body is mine. I am going to possess you, mind, body and soul," he whispered, as one finger grazed the outside of my arm.

I looked right into his eyes and not one hint of amusement in them. He looked dead serious!

I am sure I blinked and I even more sure I let out a small gasp. Not enough for the crew to hear but definitely loud enough for Guard to hear. I pulled myself together and made sure my lips were beside his ear and whispered just as quietly as he did, "I don't have time for you or anyone else. I am taking myself out of your game." I straightened up and took two steps back then turned towards the diner and walked away.

God, I hope I looked determined and strong. I didn't look back but I knew his eyes were following all the way to the diner and I also knew that his crew of men were staring and grinning. Keep walking. A few more steps and I would be inside Milly's Diner.

An hour later and I was just finishing my second cup of coffee and into my eighth conversation with Bournham patrons. It was such a quaint little place. The tables had crisp white tablecloths and the walls with a pale mint with old-fashioned table and chairs. The counters were spotless and I could see that Milly and Benny took great care of their place. Milly and I exchanged cookie recipes and chatted about the who's who of the town. Our conversation grew from just the two of us into a lively chatter of eight lively townspeople. I loved listening to the history lessons from the town. They explained how the town took a harsh financial hit a few years back and how the growth of the auto parts and specialized mechanics shop added jobs and security. Apparently this was not the only venture that is funded by the Satan's Pride MC. I also found out that MC was a Motorcycle Club not a gang. This was Guard's shop, so needless to say I was paying close attention. If you heard them speak you would think he was a super demi God. None of these people however heard him whisper that I belonged to him.

This has be rattling inside my head for the last hour. "You belong to me. Every part of your delectable body is mine. I am going to possess you, mind, body and soul."

My body still shudders when I remember his intense gaze and those words grating out in a rough whisper. Man, he was so hot. I am finally admitting it to myself. He is built, strong, lush lips and firm jaw. Let's not forget the sexy-as-hell goatee. His hand just grazed my arm and I could still feel then goose bumps forming on my arm. I shake my head back to the present moment forcing myself to pay attention to the current conversation about the town picnic and dance night. It was next Saturday night and they were looking for entertainment. I think I tuned in a little too late into the conversation however, as all eyes were on me as if they are waiting for an answer.

"Pardon?" I asked, knowing full well that I missed the entire bit.

"Why not do a choreographed dance set as part of the entertainment? It would promote your school and give people a reason to send their kid to take lessons," chimed Vi (short for Viviene). She worked at the diner and was a little younger that I. She was lively and her short red hair suited her. She was slim and full of opinion. I liked her. She reminded me a little of Becca. That would be Becca on a mission, though.

I had to admit it was a great idea. "I will need to see if I can get a dance partner to come in for next Saturday. I need to organize music keeping with the theme of your picnic and dance. There is planning involved. I don't know if I can pull it off on such short notice. I mean, I would love to and I think it's an amazing idea, Vi, I just don't know if I can get someone on such short notice," I explained.

"Well, missy, you better try! This is a great way of getting an audience just in from of you and you can't miss a chance like this. We're glad to help. The dance floor will be top notch, we can give you a ten-minute spot and we already have special-effects lights. This is perfect for you! Think of all the young girls begging their daddies to let them take lessons from the great Ava Talbot," amplified Vi.

Did I mention her high octave voice and sunshine spunk? I love this girl!

"I gotta go home and make some calls, ladies and gentlemen. Thank you for the idea," I said smartly, and I turned to Milly and Vi and asked, "Can I let you know by tomorrow afternoon if one of my partners is available?"

"You bet, girly. Head home and get it done," Milly said as she took my cup. I was putting my money on the table to pay for my coffees when she quickly said, "Put that away! First time at Milly's is on the house. It's our welcome to the family coffee."

"Thank you," I said while I kissed her cheek.

I walked out the door to head home. I was on a mission. I needed to find a way to get Brian here for this dance number. He wasn't going to make it easy. I could hear the rant about leaving New York. I can clearly have the entire conversation in my head and knew how it was going to play out. All I can do is take shot. I was biting my lip; it was a habit I had since I was a little kid whenever I was trying to come up with an answer to a problem.

Lost in my own thoughts I am completely oblivious to the Satan's Pride MC and their President and leader Guard. I may have been oblivious to Guard but his eyes followed my movements all the way back to my car. His mouth twitched and his hand went automatically to his pants making him acutely aware of his dick getting rock hard just watching me walk by.

# Chapter 2
# The Great Kiss

❝ Brian, I need your help. I know that you are still upset that I left New York and left you and Becca but I need you to look past this and help me out. I have been there for both you and Becca and I need you guys now." I ranted, and then continued with, "I just need a dance partner for Saturday night. It is a great opportunity to promote my dance school. I already have three full classes and I am getting more and more inquiries every day. One night out of your life with two songs and routines, is all I am asking. You can bring Becca and see my new place. I will make it awesome for you and Becca. I promise."

And I wait for an answer, breathing heavily after spewing out my request. Tick tock! Nothing!

"Brian, say something!" I implored.

"Okay," he replied simply.

One word.

"Okay?" I asked, in slight confusion.

"Yeah! Becca misses you and I miss you. It will give us some time together and we can see the sweet little town you keep talking about," Brian firmly stated. And then the photographer Brian took charge. "Since we are talking about favours, Ava, I really need your help too. I have a big project I landed and I need some special exclusive poses. I know you can give them to me. This contract sets Baby Duncan up for college and not only will you get your fee we can split the residual 5 percent each. It's a win/win/win for all of us. Happy client, happy us and happy you. What do you say?"

"Hey, hon, how long have you had this contract?" I teased. I know full well that Brian has been stewing on this for a while. "Nevermind! I don't care. Let's coordinate our schedules so that I don't miss any of the classes I am teaching. I'm in." Then added, "Just remember the same rules apply. I have say in what I wear and how much skin shows." I affirmed. I am very cautious when I choose my modeling jobs. I want to make sure that I am portrayed in a classy and elegant manner. As I get older I want to be remembered as a classic beauty not some slutty barmaid trying to stay in the game too long.

"Of course. We'll come down Friday afternoon; we can practice and rock your set. Becca expects your homemade pasta with your 'to die for' rose sauce," Brian said heavily accentuating the words.

"Anything she wants!" I say. "I better get moving. I have lots to do to get ready. I will send you an email with the details and map to my place."

Yippee! I have a partner and I get to see my two best friends. I quickly called Milly and confirmed that I can take part in the entertainment. She was thrilled for me too. She was organizing the stage and music so I gave her the music wanted to have played. Then I picked a routine that Brian and I performed in the past. This was during our hungry years where we both danced and competed to win prize money. This was prior to Becca and photography for him and way before modeling and James came into my life. We have gone full circle and Brian and I are dancing together again.

This was a dangerous trip down memory lane, one that will end with tears staining my cheeks and a heavy heart. I played back the last time Brian and I went out dancing with Becca in tow. After a long day in studio with Brian's first major contract we decided to celebrate with a night out together.

We sat together in a corner booth sipping our Pinot Grigio, getting up to dance whenever we heard a song that moves us. Out the corner of my eye I spotted a handsome blond man. He was looking at me and glanced away when I caught him looking, like a little boy caught with his hand in the cookie jar. He was thirty-something and he looked adorable. So for the first time ever I took the chance and made my way over to him. I extended my hand and introduced myself, and he took my hand in his, his handsome brown eyes melting into my soft green eyes and that date was the beginning of seven wonder years together.

Guard

James was sweet, gentle and calm. He loved me. There was nothing James wouldn't do to make me happy. There was a note waiting for me in the oddest places when I needed them the most. He got along well with everyone. He was a computer analyst and there were times when everyone was highly stressed. But not my James. He stayed cool and calm and told me I was his anchor. We dated for two years before we got married and have five lovely years together.

No one is perfect and of course compromises were made by both of us to make sure we always made time for one another. Our alone time was untouchable. Quiet nights on the couch sipping wine, snuggling and soft kisses. Beautiful soft kisses. Even the way he made love to me was soft, delicate; I would say he was worshiping my body. He was my first and my only lover. It was good. Loving and good.

Then in an instant, one microsecond, he was gone. A drunk driver lost control of his vehicle and veered into James' car. He was gone instantly. His light went out and so did mine. It has been so dark and lonely that I couldn't even step outside to see the sun for weeks. It hurt! It still hurts, less than it has in the past and now it has turned into emptiness and then sometimes guilt because I can't remember every moment we shared.

I wipe a tear from my eye and I force myself to back into this moment. I am here in Bournham and in my cozy cottage home. I am a dance teacher and at last count I have three classes filled. An hour later, I am in my PJ pink shorts and matching tank with little silver stars. I am about to pop in my *Speed* DVD with Keanu Reeves. Love that guy. And I am totally a Sandra Bullock fan. She is just so cool and so naturally pretty. I am twenty minutes into the movie and end up nodding off on my comfy sofa with my blanket wrapped around me.

I stretch out wondering, how morning came so fast? What am I doing on the sofa?

Arg! I fell asleep watching my movie. I hate when I do that.

First up, a hot shower, then coffee and breakfast. I dress in my black yoga pants and matching sports bra with a loose grey fitting tank overtop. My hair is in a tight, neat ponytail. I head off to my dance studio.

My studio is so cool. It opens like a garage door and as soon as the door is open it allows for a huge dance space. My closest neighbour is two miles down the road so I can crank the music and dance. My big plan is to get the routines completed for the three classes I am starting in two weeks and practicing for my Saturday performance.

11

Four hours later I am feeling pretty damn good about myself. All my classes are prepared and I have pushed myself to choreograph the final dances for the parents' recital. I think I will turn it into a BBQ night and have the parents get to know me better. This is weeks away but I am a planner. And I got to have control. Feels good!

I move to the control panel and make my song selection for one of the dances Brian and I will be performing. I want to pick something that thirty- and forty-year-olds can relate to. I wanted something classic rock with meaning. I picked "Layla" by Eric Clapton.

The soulful sound of Mr. Clapton filled the room. The guitar intro ignites and I transform. I am no longer me, I am Layla. I move my feet and body to the sound of the music. It is slow and sensual and perfectly timed with the changeup in beat and tone. My body spins and lands moving with carefree abandonment. Me and the music. Nothing else exists. I hear the words, the tortured strain of Eric's throaty voice. I move around the chair I placed in the centre of the room. Leaning into it to get the right step and shape to my body. Feeling the music and lost in my own wonderful world, until the music ends and the last cord is strummed. I end up with my body over the chair bent backward with my back arched and with one hand centred on the seat supporting the rest of my body. Feet perfectly aligned with my other arm straight back taking my body into a full stretch. To an audience the intention is to paints a picture of a woman in the highest moment of abandonment.

I hear clapping and whistles. What the fuck? I jump out of my pose and turn my head. I see big burly biker guy with Vi hanging onto his arm. Next to them I see a slighter shorter biker dude, no less intimidating with hands on hips grinning with a raised eye. Both of which I had seen before in front of the mechanic shop. But more frightening than any of this is Guard standing against the door a few feet away. His eyes were a wild blue and his arms were strained and tense and his jaw drawn tight. It seems like he was trying to get himself under control. What the hell is he mad at?

I must have said, "What the fuck?" out loud. I think I surprised Vi. She giggled and came up to hug me.

"That was amazing, Ava. You are unbelievable," she said still hugging me.

I was still a little surprised but hugged her back and asked, "What are you doing here?"

My eyes moved to the three men still staring at me like I was a new item on a takeout menu, and moved my eyes back to Vi.

"Some of the guys were curious about the great new friend I have been talking about and they wanted to meet you," she replied. She sounded so pleased that her friends were interested and protective of her.

"I'm sorry, Vi. Did you not think that perhaps I would feel unsafe with three strangers walking up to my home?" I asked a little annoyed. I know I sounded cold but I couldn't help it. I was feeling invaded and uncomfortable.

"Oh, honey, you have it wrong. Let me introduce you to *my* awesome man and our motorcycle brothers," she says and she steps away from me towards big burly dude first. Vi wraps her arms around him and he protectively tucks her into his side. "This is my old man, Orion," she chirps.

My eyes move to Orion and I notice the slight smile on his lips.

"Hey," he grunts.

"Um...hey," I replied. He didn't look like an "old man." Maybe he carried his age well?

Vi turned her attention to the shorter biker to their right. He was a good-looking guy although he looked a little haunted. I felt that his eyes had seen more than anyone should ever have to see. His dark eyes and curly dark hair matched his very fit and tattooed arms.

"This is Demon," she added.

My eyes met Demon's and he did not speak and I got a chin nudge. His way of say hello, I guess.

"Hey," I said quietly.

"I can introduce myself, Vi," I heard a sultry smooth voice behind me.

He was right behind me. I turn around to find Guard so very close to me. I force myself to look up into his face. My God he was gorgeous. My eyes met his and he reached out to take my hand. All I could do is watch as he tagged my hand and pulled me closer to him. God, I hope I was still breathing. I twisted my head around to look for Vi, Orion and Demon.

"They're not here, my little dancer." The sexy growl pulled me closer still.

Guard placed my hands on his chest in an attempt to keep some space between us. No such luck as he wrapped his arms around my waist and trapped my hands between us. I was full on against his chest at this point. I pull my head back to meet his gaze. I should say something but my mouth couldn't formulate words.

I finally find my voice and ask, "Why are you here?" I muttered and unconsciously bit my lower lip waiting for an answer.

"Baby, I told you already. You're mine. You had to expect that I would be coming to claim you." He says this as one of his hand holds my waist firm and the other navigates its way tingling up my spine to rest at the back of my head. His head dips close to mine. His nose moves along mine intimately. His lips caress my cheek making a path to my ear. "So beautiful."

My breath hitches as I try to get my betraying body under control. No man has been this close to me since James. I drop my gaze, lowering my eyes in an attempt to hide my arousal. I try to push my hands away from his rock-hard chest.

"Hush, baby," he whispers at my ear. "Let me hold you."

Oh. My. God. I am losing this battle. I can't think straight. I can hear his breath in my ear. His hand at the back of my head holds me firm and tilts my head back exposing my neck. His lips move from my ear down the side of my neck. Guard's lips hit this sensitive spot right under my ear and a soft moan leaves my throat. I bite my lip again in a desperate attempt to ground myself.

No, no, no.

"Look at me angel," he commanded. My eyes met his and I see this strong fire in his eyes. "I'm taking your mouth, baby. I need to taste you."

Oh, no, no, no. I try to push at his chest halfheartedly purely for self-preservation.

His lips run along mine and he presses his to mine. His tongue licks my lips and I gasp and my eyes drift closed once again. Taking full advantage, his tongue explores my mouth. I take the ride along with Guard. He set the pace and power of our kiss. He presses closer and my hands are now fisted into his t-shirt holding on tight to bury myself deeper into him. One arm at my waist moves up to grip my head and with his hands on either side of my head and his lips moving sensually along mine and his tongue dancing with mine, I have lost all control. Long, slow, sweet, deep kiss. It has been so very long since I've had that kind of kiss and none were quite as extraordinary as this one.

Finally when I thought I was going to pass out from the shear intensity of our kiss, he pulls his lips away from mine ever so gently. Our breathing is hard and ragged. My eyes flutter open. I can feel the heat coming off our bodies.

Did that just happen? I stayed quiet, lowered my head and stared at my hands still tightly gripping his t-shirt. I open my palms and try to step back and I am immediately pulled back to his chest jerk my head up. He was grinning and not that sweet and cute little grin but that cocky "I'm gonna get some" grin.

"Um....ah...." I am speechless. What is wrong with me? I am not a sixteen-year-old girl with her first crush.

"Beautiful," he muttered and lowered his lips to mine and softly brushed and licks his lips over mine. "You belong to me. You understand what I'm saying?"

"Um, not really," I mumbled against his lips. "Please let me go. I got caught up in the moment. I'm sorry. You need to let me go now." I tried once again to pull away and I couldn't even budge him. Not even a little.

His arms holding me steadfast, as he informed me, "Oh, no, little angel, you are not retreating back into the ice cold shell. I like you soft and warm and in my arms." He continued talking softly but firmly. "I can't wait to have you in my bed, under me, moaning and gasping until you scream my name when you come."

I'm stunned.

How do I respond to that? Besides stating the obvious and shaking my head. "That's not possible. I'm not dating anyone. I have a business to get off the ground." I was ready to continue my rant and noticed that he stopped paying attention and was strumming his finger along the tip of my ear. I stopped talking. His hands are distracting, my head is getting muddled.

"Angel, you think this is an option, to hide from me, I am informing you that it's not. Let me make this clear for you. I am staking my claim and you are mine. I am giving you some time to adjust to the situation. I am being sensitive to the fact that you have probably never been with someone like me. Make no mistake, you are mine."

Wow, seriously! I have no choice?! Kinda hot, actually.

Have I lost my mind? Get some control, I urge myself. I opened my mouth to inform him of his need to seek psychiatric attention.

Before I could say a word he placed a finger to my lips and continued, "We are going to explore this and you are going love every fucking minute of this ride."

Well, fuck! Now I am getting a little annoyed. I pull out of his arms, and stumble back.

"I don't think you have the right to tell me who I do or do not date. I think it's a bit presumptuous to assume I'll sleep with you. You are talking crazy! You need to seek help."

Uh-oh! I think I angered the beast. He steps purposely towards me and I begin to walk backward right into Orion. Vi and Demon were close behind. He steadies me so that I don't topple over and let's go immediately.

His gaze meets Guard's and says, "Got the call, gotta ride and it's got to be now."

The two men exchange looks as I am digesting their biker code lingo. I am gripped by the arm and hauled back to Guard's side.

He snakes his arm around my waist and pulls me to face him and his mouth comes down hard crushing mine and sliding his tongue deep into my mouth. I soften under his mouth. I am powerless when he kisses me like that. And as quickly as it started it came to an end. He pulls his head back and directs his attention to his companions while tucking me into his side. I am completely bewildered. Shocked into silence.

"Let's head out. Make the call and let the others know where to meet up," he directed.

Then he tilts my head up with a firm finger under my chin. "Mine! Everyone knows this and you need to get this. I'll be back in a couple of days. Hear me when I say this, you belong to me."

He moves his lips against my swollen ones whispering, "Soon, my angel. Very soon. My patience is limited."

Guard and his entourage mount their rides and ride off. I am still standing in my studio, my fingertips running along my swollen lips, trying to make sense of what the hell just happened.

# Chapter 3
# BFFs

I t's been days since Guard came to see me. He hasn't been back and I wasn't sure how I felt about this. My head tells me I to be relieved but truth be told I am little disappointed. It's not like I have been waiting by the front door ready to run into his arms the minute he got off his bike. I have had plenty to keep me busy getting ready for classes and making sure I have the routine perfect for tomorrow's night festivities. I was completely freaked at what would happen if he showed yet my mind went back to those kisses. I have never been kissed like that before. I have never felt my body lose complete control over a kiss.

Brian and Becca were on their way in today. The last text from Becca let me know that they would be another hour, with little x's and o's after her name. Adorable! That was at 6:15, almost forty-five minutes ago.

I was taking full advantage of my kitchen tonight. The sauce was simmering, and the homemade pasta was all prepped and ready to be tossed into the boiling water when the timing was right. A fresh French loaf and crisp green salad was on the menu as well; however, I knew that apple pie was Becca's favourite and so she shall have it.

Becca and I rarely indulged when we modeled but we knew how to appreciate a delicious piece of apple pie on occasion. With Becca in her sixth month and fully into the throes of motherhood indulgence I was going to make sure I spoiled her.

I heard the bell while upstairs. I was just getting changed and I zipped down the stairs in yoga short-shorts and oversized tank top. I whipped the door open to let them in and found myself face to face with Guard. His arms braced on either of the door frame; his body took up the entire space. I took a step back, really surprised to see him. I am sure my mouth was hanging open.

He took off his shades and slowly perused me starting from the top of my head, lingering on my breasts, slowly moving his eyes down my body taking in my legs and manicured barefoot toes. Then he started from the bottom and worked his way back up to meet my eyes.

Oh, man! He looked good. I mean really, really good. Tight faded blue jeans and black t-shirt that showed off his defined muscles, he looked yummy. His tattoos on display where is t-shirt sleeve ends.

My eyes drift to his face. He looked amused. A little smile played his face as I stood there like an idiot staring.

"Nice to know my angel missed me. I heard you running down the stairs to greet me. That's sweet, baby," he said and started walking towards me.

I put my hand up as if to stop him. An instinctive gesture and highly ineffective, I might add.

My hand was flattened against his chest. I quickly said, "Wait!" in a shaky voice.

Guard stopped moving forward but snaked his arm around my waist to hold me there.

I kept going at a really, really fast pace, I might add, "I have friends coming in from New York and they are going to be here any minute now. I can't have this discussion about what you think about you and I, or your crazy 'mine' mentality. We have had less than half an hour together in total. And frankly, I think you are a little batty. I'm not going to lie and say that the kiss wasn't nice, it was but we are so very different and I don't want what I can't handle. I am sure that there are plenty of women out there that are more equipped to handle the likes of you," I babbled. "And most importantly, please let me have an evening with my best friends. I haven't seen them since I've moved here and I miss them." I know I sounded sentimental and girly but I didn't care. I am sure I had tears welding in my eyes at this point but I didn't care. This is how I felt and I didn't do pretense all that well.

His smile turned into a chuckle and he held my waist tighter, pulling me a little closer. He lowered his forehead to mine, and said, "Give me a kiss, angel, and I'll leave to have your girl time."

# Guard

Do I tell him that Brian isn't a girl? It isn't any of his business, really. But I couldn't stop my mouth from spewing out more.

"Um…well…in the spirit of full disclosure my best friends are a couple. Brian and Becca. Brian has been my dance partner for years and Becca and I have been friends since we started modeling together," I informed him. Now I was completely weirding myself out because I don't have to explain anything to anyone and I am doing it anyway.

"Glad you told me, angel. I would be have been pissed to find out some guy was sleeping here with you. The only man allowed being in your bed is me." He was grinning and teasing me. Openly teasing me!

The nerve! I was rambling like an idiot and he was smirking like the cat with a bowl of cream. That did it!

"You don't get to decide that," I injected and my hand turned into a pointed finger stabbing him in the chest. He had the innate ability to push my buttons!

"Angel, I do have a say. Being mine means just that," he informed me in a low husky voice. "I do see your point, though, about not spending enough time together. I think I should stay for dinner and meet your friends," I was informed. "A little time together with my sweet girl and her friends sounds like a perfect night."

My head jerked up. He wants to meet my friends. I know this isn't a good idea. My friends are preppy prenatal parents and I am going to introduce them to a biker dude. A gorgeous, hot male specimen but still a biker!

Wide-eyed panic hits.

"I…um…I'm not so sure that would be a good idea."

Oh, my God! Too late! Brian's car is driving up the driveway and there is no way Guard's going anywhere.

I let out a heavy sigh. "Okay, you can stay but they are going to think we are together and they have this thing about protecting me." I continued blathering with my hands moving and gesturing. "Shit! I don't have time to go through all this. I just ask that you please be nice to them or they are going to make my life crazier than it already is. And their brand of crazy almost rivals yours."

I was shaking my head and I know I had wild eyes and my lips were trembling. Guard was looking right at me and pulled me close and kissed me lightly on the lips.

Then whispered, "Don't worry, angel, I will look after you. It'll be just fine," as he squeezed me in an effort to comfort me.

"Ava! What the hell!" Becca exclaimed.

I moved my head around Guard's shoulder and I found myself in full view of a very pregnant Becca with her mouth hanging open and her hand running through her hair, telltale sign that she is stunned and confused.

I dropped my head on Guard's should and groaned quietly. I can feel his body shaking with laughter.

I could hear Brian asking Becca, "Becs, what are you doing standing at the door? Move in, honey. These bags are heavy. You packed enough for a month."

Guard turned to face both Becca and Brian, and moved me to his side and slid me close. That's when Brian looked past Becca to see me snagged close to Guard with his arm around me.

"Holy hell! Did hell just freeze over?" Brian bellowed. A warm smile crossed his face though. Then he stared at his wife still in shock. "Becca, come on, honey, take a few more steps so that I can set the bags down."

He nudged his wife further in the door. Becca moved in another few steps still open-mouthed.

Guard finally let go of me and reached around and took a suitcase from Brian. "Can I give you a hand?"

Brian let go of it and replied, "Thanks, man."

I pulled Becca farther into the room moving her out of the traffic of suitcases. I hugged my friend and she came out of her shocked state and hugged me back. Then she said, "You have some explaining to do, Ava." She did not do this softly or quietly but with steely determination.

"Becs, move over and let me hug our runaway friend," Brian teased and gently moved his wife out of the way and moved in for a giant bear hug and kissed me on the cheek. "So, turtle, anything you want to tell us?" he teased as he pulled back watching me turn a bright shade of pink.

"Turtle?" I hear this come from Guard.

"You have noticed how our lovely Ava tends to separate herself away from most people and events." Brian said, "So I started calling her turtle in hopes that she gets my point that she shy away from life and hide like a turtle in its shell."

I wish I had an actual shell. Guard was smiling at Brian's interpretation of me. Brian was proud of enlightening my so-called "boyfriend" about me, and Becca was standing there tapping her toe waiting for an explanation of Guard.

# Guard

I stared at the faces of Becca and Brian, both waiting for answers and then ran my eyes over to Guard. I must have looked completely lost because Guard came to stand behind me and slipped his hands around my waist. I instinctively went to place my hands over his and looked over my shoulder to look at him. I was glad he did because I had no idea how I was still standing.

Guard spoke before I could react, which was a good thing 'cause I couldn't for the life think of how I was going to explain him. What could I say? Meet the man who thinks he owns me although we have shared all of two kisses and one very odd conversation.

"Sorry, guys, we thought we had a few more minutes of alone time. Our timing sucks." Then he bends down and brushes his lips against mine. "Angel, introduce me to your friends," he urged.

I turn my head to Brian and Becca facing to smirking grins. "Becca and Brian, my two very best friends, meet Guard," I said quietly.

Leave it to Becca to push it. "Ava, honey, and who is Guard?" she asked, still tapping her toe.

Guard spoke up. "I thought it was kind of obvious but I am Ava's man," dipping down to kiss my cheek.

Oh, boy! Let the chaos begin!

Becca screeched! "Oh, yea! Woo-hoo! Bri, did you hear that?" Then she jumped over and pulled me away from Guard and hugged me again.

Kill me now! Guard must be loving this. Who knows what he's thinking?

"Becca, baby, calm down. All this jumping around is not good for you or my baby. Quit yelling, babe, you are going to burst our eardrums," Brian said as he kisses his wife's cheek. Then he turned to Guard. "Nice to meet you, man. Sorry for the crazy female, hormones and shit. Gotta say this is a bit of a shock. No fuckin' clue how the hell you managed to penetrate the deep freeze called Ava but I am fucking glad you did."

I groan loudly. They are talking about me like I am not even in the same room. Bring the attention back to me. FUCK! This is going to be a long night.

I extricate myself from the room announcing that I need to get dinner ready. I busied myself in the kitchen with Becca while the guys went out on the terrace to chat. This makes me very nervous. I am going to let myself think it's about sports and cars and whatever else guys talk about. Although I hurried myself so that I could get them all in the same room so I could do damage control.

I called them to the table set with simple white plates with a silver edging, crystal glasses and delicious loads amounts of food.

Guard poured wine for the three of us and I bought sparking nonalcoholic cider for Becca. No reason she can't pretend! Dinner was nice, I moved the conversation to the new baby and that was a hot topic so I was good. Then I asked Brian about the projects he has on the go and that was great because Brian is so passionate about his work.

I kept glancing over to Guard and he seemed genuinely interested in the conversations at the table. Either he was a really good actor or he liked my best buds. He asked questions and went with the flow of chatter. He smiled and squeezed my knee under the table several times. He even helped clear the table.

That's when I noticed...I was smiling! I was actually smiling. It has been a long time since I was actually smiling.

We all gathered to the terrace for coffee and warm apple pie. I made sure to add an extra whopping dollop of ice cream on Becca's. My reward for that was, "So how did you two meet?"

And the interrogation begins.

"We met in town. Ava was in her own little world and I decided to rattle her cage." Guard laughed.

"I think I handled my own," I informed them. I kept my eyes on my coffee cup.

"Yeah, angel, you did. That's why I won't let you go. I saw a flash of fire in those very mysterious eyes." Guard lightly touched my hand and entwined his hand in mine. Then he directed his attention to my pals and asked, "Ava hasn't told me too much about her early years. Either one of you want to give me an 'Ava story'?"

OH, NO! Open season on Ava! I jolted in my seat.

"I'm sure that they are tired and don't need the trip down memory lane," I said quickly, too quickly.

Becca piped up. "Ooh, I'll tell you our happy meeting story. The expression on your face when we met and it was priceless." She loved this stuff. The emotional bonding and touchy feely has been even more prominent since she was pregnant.

Oh, damn! Here it comes. I sigh and place my head in my hands. "I beg you both, please don't."

To no avail, and then she started.

"Ava was hired for a photo shoot. This was her first one and she was nervous because she had never modeled. It was freaking her out since most models start doing this at fourteen and she had just turned twenty. The ad company wanted her because she was fresh and she could dance and they wanted action shots and an exotic look. I was hired because we are complete opposites. Different coloring, Ava mysterious and I am classic model. She walks in all quiet and just nods and listens. They hand the clothes they want her to model. She moves into the dressing room and let loose a 'Hell no!' She absolutely refused to come out wearing them. They asked me to go talk to her and calm her down. They really wanted her or they would have shown her the door. I asked she would let me in." For added effect Becca hold up her hands, waving them enthusiastically, "Took me ten minutes to convince her to open the door. I think she looked hot!" Then Becca looks right at me. "You rocked those jeans and the sequin blue bra."

Major groan! I hear Guard opening laughing and Brian joining in.

Turning back to Guard. "Ava refused to walk around half naked. She was really upset and said she would gladly walk away from the shoot if they insisted on that bra. She looked so sad and when she said that although she needed the funds there was no way she could pose in that bra I left the dressing room and told them I wanted to wear the bra and threw a little hissy fit reminding them that I am the main model for the shoot. The top they had picked out for me was backless but still covered everything and I got Ava to agree that it covered more skin. We switched and she finally came out." Then she face got soft and sweet. "Best part of the whole day was when they turned on the lighting and music for mood and Ava danced. She was spectacular and I could see why they chose her. We played around on set all day and ended up laughing a lot. I asked her to come out with me dancing that night at a club. Ava told me that she and her friend Brian were dancing in a competition. They needed the prize money so I asked if I could come along. That's when I met my gorgeous hubby. Of course, I saw Brian and fell in love."

I had no idea that when she said "friends" she actually meant "friends." I wanted to rip her hair out!

"Becca!" I gasped. "What the hell! You never told me that. I kept telling you we were friends, over and over again."

"Sure, how was I going to admit I was jealous of a sweet little dancer? I was a seasoned model and there was no way I was going to let on," she said indignantly.

I can feel Guard's eyes on me. "You modeled, angel? Do you still model?" His fingertips grazed over my shoulder blaze in a lazy pattern; a very intimate touch.

I lifted my eyes to his. "Yes, I still do some modeling. Very infrequently and only with specific photographers. Brian is one of five that I still choose to work with."

Brian piped up. "We have a shoot set for next week. Ava's agreed to help me out. My clients want some special glamorous looks and I know I can get Ava to give me that." Turning to me Brian continues. "I have the designs for the clothing in my bag. Remind me to show them to you tomorrow for approval."

"Okay," I mumbled. I was finding it really hard to concentrate with Guard running is fingers over me. "How did you and my angel meet?" Guard nodded over to Brian.

"I am going to give you the abbreviated version. We both were in a performance academy. My parents are assholes, no love lost there. Ava's parents had just passed away in the accident. She was so lost and I was so angry. They matched us to dance together. Poor Ava. I was a complete and utter jerk to her. I was in my own hell. I couldn't focus and concentrate. I bruised her so many times just because my head wasn't in the game. I have no idea how many times I dropped her day after day. Shit, it was weeks before she utterly lost it on me. Ava walks up to me at practice and told me to get my head out of my ass. She has a way of making me talk about my past, and she never judged. She genuinely wanted me to be happy and took the time to get to know about all sides of me. We practiced more and joined forces to win competitions to pay for school. We've been through a whole lot of crap." Brian took a deep breath.

And then the hammer dropped. "James, death almost killed her. We are so glad that she met you, Guard," Becca said softly.

"Oh, my God! Stop! No more Ava stories," I said. My heart was racing and I wasn't prepared to talk about James our marriage or my guilt.

"Hey, honey, what's wrong?" a concerned Becca said.

"It's been a long day, Bec."

"Actually you need to get your rest, Becs, and Ava and I have a day of practice for this dance set tomorrow so I need to get some sleep." He turns to Guard. "I hope you are ready for Ava's heavenly waffles with homemade cream," Brian interjected.

"You bet. Wouldn't miss it," Guard says smoothly.

They all get up to say goodnight. What is he staying here? Really!

Brian and Becca head towards the guest room.

"Angel, you look wiped. I'll clear off the rest of the dishes. Why don't you head up?" Guard pulls me out of my chair and moves me towards the stairs.

I take the time to wash my face and compose myself. I brush my teeth and work through my nightly routine mechanically all the time thinking what the hell just happened down there.

I have to admit, Guard was polite, sweet to Becca, spent time getting to know Brian, and cleared the dishes. Who the hell was this man? This man is sweet and gentle. My head is even more befuddled. I don a pair of yellow PJ shorts with a drawstring and a matching tank. I head out into my bedroom.

I walk out to see Guard half naked with only his jeans. My mouth watered he is so sexy. This is the first time I get to see his impressive chest. Hard abs, all muscle, and an intricate pattern of tattoos adorning his body. I hope my mouth is closed.

"Angel, come here," a deep tough voice rumbles, shaking me out of my daze.

"Um...."

"Baby, come here."

"Um...."

"Ava, here, baby."

I walked over to him. His arms come around me. "We have to make time to talk shit out. Not tonight, baby, but soon."

What? What are we going to talk about?

"Um...."

"Not tonight, babe. Get in bed. I'll be right there." He stroked my back lightly. "Guard, I'm not sure this is a good idea. Maybe you should...."

"No way, angel. You're not pushing me out. I got a taste of the real Ava tonight and I want to know all of her. We are not having this out tonight baby. Get in bed, I'll be right there." His hands are in my hair, tilting my face upward, and sensually rubbing his nose across my mine and letting his lips run over my cheek, then brushing my lips.

I take a deep breath. "Okay."

I make my way to my bed and catch Guard moving towards the bathroom. I make my way under the covers, sitting up in bed. I was lost in my own thoughts about the events of the evening when a short while later, Guard joins me and his hands go to his jean, I turn my head. I hear the zipper drop and feel the covers pull back and he climbs in beside me.

I lie on my side away my back to his front. I feel Guard's arm wrap around my waist. I tense in his arms.

"Angel, relax. You are too tense, baby." His lips nuzzle my neck; he pulls me closer to him. I make a move to move away. "Hush, angel, let me hold you."

Sounds so nice. It's been so long since I was held like this. I feel safe in Guard's warm.

"Mmm...."

We are going to have to talk but for right now I am going to revel in the strength of his arms, and a few minutes later I fall asleep.

# Chapter 4
## You Share, I Share

I woke in the middle of the night. Not uncommon for me. What is uncommon is the feel of a heavy arm over my waist pinning me to the bed and legs wrapped around mine. The sounds of deep breathing confirming he is soundly asleep and I am encased in his arms.

Turning my head I see Guard huddled close spooning me in a deep sleep. I don't want to wake him. I try to move away, just to have his arm tighten and pull me closer so I try to settle back to sleep.

A few minutes later, I am still wide awake.

Half-hour later, still nothing.

I have to get up. I am getting antsy. I slowly and careful untangle myself from Guard and make my way to the terrace off the bedroom, wrapping myself in a throw at the foot of the bed. I spend many hours sitting and staring at the sky. Sleep has been elusive to me since I lost my parents and even more so since I lost James. I am not out there very long at all when Guard comes to stand at the doorway.

"Can't sleep?" he asks with a husky sleepy voice.

I turn to look at him. "I have trouble sleeping. I have had it for years. I am sorry if I woke you. Go back to bed, Guard, please."

"Come back to bed." He extended his hand.

"I'll just keep you up. Really, I'm fine here. I do this almost every night."

"Angel, you either come to bed or I am carrying you there." His voice was determined.

I must have hesitated too long because I found myself scooped out of my chair and being hauled back in bed. He settled back in bed sitting up with pillows propped behind him and hauled me up to sit between his legs with my back against his front, arms wrapped tight around me.

"What's keeping you up?" he whispered in my ear.

"My mind just keeps moving. It's nothing. I left everything to come here," I whispered back, not too convincingly.

"Baby, we can do this one of two ways. You can come clean and just tell me what's moving in your head or I continue to poke and prod until I think I got it all. Personally I don't care either way. I can kiss it out of you or you can tell me and I will kiss you after. What's it going to be, Ava?" he informed me. He kissed the back of my neck.

"I don't think I want to share. I don't know you and you are demanding a lot from me. Why don't you tell me about your past?" I bit back.

"All right, let's play, angel." He strummed his fingers up and down my arms calmly. "You ask a question, I answer and then I ask a question and you answer. Seem fair?" His voice was soft and sweet, almost hypnotic.

How very logical? How do I argue with that? He sounds so sincere and sweet.

"Who goes first?" I whisper.

"Angel first." I can feel his lips curve upwards against my hair.

"Why are you here?" I asked hesitantly.

"You are soft and strong. You fight me because you feel you have to not because you want to. You are loyal, and fiery. I see how you protect Becca and how you love them both. Your mouth is delicious and your body makes me hard just looking at it. I want to know more and I want to explore us," he stated firmly. Doing it right next to my ear so I can hear every one clearly and feel his warm breath brush over me like a blanket.

WOW! Fuck, that was nice.

"Who's James, Ava?"

I knew that was going to be the question. I took a deep breath and exhaled. I looked down where our hands were connected at my waist. I took another breath.

"Talk to me, angel." He nudged to move his lips to my neck and kissed me lightly.

"He was my husband. He was killed by a drunk driver," I said quietly. Then I continued. "He was a good man. Kind, sweet, and gentle. He loved me." I corrected, "No, he adored me."

"I'm sorry, baby. How long ago, angel?" Guard asked nuzzling his jaw against me neck.

"Three years ago," I breathed. "I am sure you figured out I have not dated since. This scares me," I admitted.

I could feel a tear drop from my cheek and hit Guard's arm. He turned so that he could look at me and kissed away the next tear that started to run down my cheek.

Then he kissed my lips lightly. He continued to placed feather light kisses on my face and down my neck then moved me to lay beside him, moving me to his side with his arm around me and my arm thrown over his lean stomach, my head on his shoulder.

"Hush, angel. Enough for tonight. Close your eyes, baby."

And I did.

# Chapter 5

# Dancing or Dueling

My eyelids lifted slowly and found myself alone in my bed. I looked over to the bathroom and no sign of Guard there either. I heard the rumbling of voices downstairs in the kitchen. I pulled on my jeans and red ribbed tank top and raced down the stairs. I turned the corner to find my BFFs and Guard sipping coffee nattering away with one another.

"Mornin', angel." Guard came 'round the counter and planted a full on kiss with tongue. Oh, boy, he tasted good. He smells good and he looks great.

"Mornin'," I said a little breathless. "Need coffee."

"Not a morning girl?" he teased and reached over me to the cupboard to get me a mug and filled it with coffee.

"Nah-uh," I muttered. I reached for the milk and splashed it into my coffee, taking a good long first sip.

"Morning, Ava," chirped Becca. "Did you sleep well?" She looks so bright and bushy tailed. I wish she would l stop being so sweet and perky.

"Um, mornin'. Just let me have two more sips before you keep going," I grunted.

"Poor turtle. Becs, you know you don't get anything out of her until she's had at least two cups of coffee," Brian teased.

"With all due respect to you both, bite me!" I glared at Brian and Becca. The both snickered. I then turned to Guard and said, "You gave me coffee, so thank you."

31

"Does this mean we don't get waffles?" Guard laughed and Brian and Becca joined in.

Fifteen minutes and two cups of coffee later I was making waffles and rhyming off the songs I picked for Brian and I to dance to tonight.

"Layla by Clapton I can understand, but Cheerleader?! What? Why?" Brian asked clearly confused with my choices. Guard was choking down a swig of coffee at Brian look of disgust and started howling.

"We are catering to parents and kids. I need one modern pop hit to attract the kids and the other that the parents can relate with. You have any other suggestions I am open but they have to work with the core steps we have already decided on and no time to change outfits so we have to pick something that works for both. I am open for suggestions," I explained.

"You got it lined up?" Brian asked, wanting to know if I had it available to play on the stereo and I nodded. "Play it."

I hit the control and keyed up the song. Halfway through, he turned down the volume and vetoed my selection. "Okay, whatcha got to replace it? Remember, kid friendly and new!" I threw back at him.

I continued making waffles and directing them to the table while Becca, Brian and Guard went through the list of music. They settled on Uptown Funk by Bruno Mars.

"I'm good with that. We start with Uptown Funk and end with Layla. Sound good," Brian agreed. "Right. Outfits?" he inquired.

Becca piped up, since she was our resident fashionista. "I think you keep it simple. Jean and tight white t-shirt with black boots for Brian and Ava do you still have the cutoff jean short and frayed black shirt? Ooh and add the black leather hat. That would be hot! Oh, and the ankle boots with the high heels for effect," she kept babbling on. She is totally in her element here.

"I'm not sure that would be appropriate," I said. "It might be too much. We're not in New York anymore. This is a small town and I don't want to offend any parents."

"Angel, don't you need to rehearse? Do a dress rehearsal and try it on. We'll tell you what we think," Guard said. Then he added, "You and Brian go get changed. Becca and I will load the dishwasher and meet you in the studio. And because I am so damn sweet I will bring you another coffee," Guard said with a grin.

Bossy, cheeky and adorably sweet!

# Guard

It wasn't long before Brian and I found our rhythm in the studio. Brian rocked his jeans and t-shirt but I was still having a problem with the shorts and shirt. Maybe I am just being self-conscious around Guard in it. Too much showing and my breasts although completely covered are very prominently shown off.

"It's hot!" Brian stated.

"They're too short for a family event. The shirt frays are too deep. You can notice too much up top. I can live with the boots and I love the hat," I countered.

Just then Becca and Guard came out.

"WOW, Ava! You rock that outfit," Becca said with excitement.

I looked at Guard to see what he thought. He was very quiet. His eyes darkened, the muscles in his arms had tensed and a sexy smile came across his face.

"Too much?" I asked, tilting my head to one side.

"Fuck me! You look fuckin' amazing." Guard liked it! "Come here, baby."

I walked over to the edge of the dance floor where he was standing. As soon as I got within arms reached he pulled me into him, one hand on my ass and the other tilting me head to one side and his mouth covering mine in a long, wet, tongue meeting tongue kiss. Full on sensual kiss that went on and on.

"Honey, they're so cute," Becca squealed.

Thus bringing me back to the studio. I broke away, breathless. Oh, my!

Guard whispers, "Wear this for me tonight."

I nodded. I couldn't formulate words. He must be a magician, I never behave like this.

It seems that more company was coming when riders drove up my driveway. As they approached, I recognized Orion and Demon. The new addition was younger, maybe mid-twenties. A very handsome biker, not rugged but model material hot. I heard Orion call him War. Doesn't suit him since he looked so fine.

As the guys approached I got my traditional "hey" and chin-jerk action. I also noticed then looking my outfit up and down.

Guard growled, "There a reason you're ogling my woman?" His arm instinctively pulls me close to his side.

Orion replied, "Nice shorts."

"You want to keep you cock, I suggest you shut it," Guard retorted.

Oh, my! My face went a deep pink. So much for sweet.

"I'm going to practice," I said and left the scene. Not my circus, not my monkeys! I have way too much to do to prepare for tonight.

Brian and I did a couple of runs before Guard walked back in. "Angel, I have to go back for a meeting. I will see you tonight. I will be there to see you dance, baby. I'll text you later today." Then he directed his attention to Brian, "Can you drive Ava down?" To which he nodded.

"How can you text me? You don't have my number," I whispered.

"Yeah, baby, I do. I programmed your number in my phone and mine in yours." He walked over to me. "Baby, I gotta go, give me a kiss." Another sweet soft kiss and he was gone.

Brian and I practiced for the rest of the morning into the afternoon. The set was perfect and we were so familiar with one another that all flowed easily.

Becca and Brian were leaving straight after the set tonight so that Brian could prepare for a client meeting, so they repacked the car and I made snacks and sandwiches. I wanted to make sure they didn't have to stop along the way if they were so set on leaving and making it back on time.

We also had the time to talk. Really talk. Both Becca and Brian lectured me. "We want you to be happy and we really like Guard," Becca said. Then Becca went to have a nap Brian let me in on what he was thinking.

"Turtle, don't shut down. He brightens your face and I saw some real smiles not that fake shit you put on your face. I haven't seen you smile in three years," Brian confessed. "Babe, don't shut down anymore. Let us in. We've missed you and Becca and I want and need you in our lives. We'll even let your badass dude in the fold," he teased.

"I'm trying, Brian." I hugged him hard. "I don't know where this is going with Guard. I'm scared and he is so intense most of the time."

"A guy gets that intense if he really wants something. It's clear he has a thing for you, Ava. Give the guy a shot at making you happy," he said. "Turtle, you deserve happy. Open up."

Advice from the one person who knew me best. Okay, I am going to try to "open up."

The town was lit up for the festivities. The main street was closed off and a main stage was setup. Lights all around, it was absolutely charming. It looked like a movie set from Disney with all the stars and lights around the grounds. The band they hired is really good. They had a mix of new and older music and little something for everyone. They had a section dedicated to rides and games. The stage holding the band was opposite to that area.

I easily found Milly and had our music selection changed. She was awesome and made me feel at ease about asking; when I know her mind must be busy with a hundred other details. Told me not to worry and would make it happen. Loving Milly more and more.

The entire town must have some out for this luau. I reconnected with everyone I met at the diner except Vi. Then it became introductions to everyone else. Most of these people had kids and many of them are girls and their mommies were so excited about a dance school for their little princesses. So I schmoozed and smiled and make contacts. They are not kidding when they say that everyone one knows everyone in this town. I saw Molly and her hubby (my first interaction with my little town-mates) and had a nice chat about how great Eddie treated me; all the while, introducing Becca and Brian to my town.

They seemed to be having a really good time. Brian made sure that mamma-to-be had all the junk food she wanted. He was so sweet he tried to win a stuffed bear for her at the games and failed miserable so decided to pay for the bear and give it to her anyway.

There were games for the kids, cotton candy, lots of food with laughter.

I didn't see Guard anywhere. I didn't see any of the Satan's Pride MC bikers. I was really hoping to see Vi. I hadn't seen her since she brought Guard over the first time. I was a little peeved that day and I wanted to make amends. I saw the lights on in the building belonging to Satan's Pride.

I guess they weren't joiners.

Milly came to find me and let me know we were on in ten minutes. Brian and I stood behind the stage stretching out and doing our last minute run through and basically getting in the zone. We both laughed about the exclusive memories we shared from way back when this was our main method of making extra money and the hilarious stories about some of the crazy couples we met along the way. Most of these couples were actually dating and when they were happy, their dancing was amazing but when there was trouble in paradise it definitely showed up in a not-so-positive light. I always told Brian that this is why we did so well. We were friends and we were able to stay friends.

This has to go well. I just spent the last two hours talking up my dance studio and had so many potential students waiting for a spectacular performance. I want and need more classes to fill to really make a go of the dance school.

Game on!

Deep breath.

We sachet onto the stage with attitude and style! Dance is all about attitude and owning the stage. Grabbing the audience attention and keeping it was harder than it looked. You want them to get into the dance with you. The lights hit the music starts and the Hip Hop beat of Uptown Funk takes off. We work it perfectly. The steps were quick and lively. Our bodies moved in perfect unison and it certainly showed our connection as partners. The kids along the stage were dancing along and the audience was clapping to the beat of the music. We kicked ass! The roar of the crowd was awesome. Brian looked at Becca backstage and was rewarded with a kisses being blown his way. I twirl in one direction to the left of Brian and bowed then move back with another twirl. That's when I noticed Guard and a huge group of Satan's Pride brothers five feet from the stage under one of the light.

He winks at me. His arms are crossed and sexy smile and in a power stance with one hand on his hips and the other in the loop of his jeans. I bow gracefully, my eyes meeting his. The music started to "Layla" and both Brian and I move into character. We tell the story of how a woman brings a man down to his knees. Slow, sensual movements; precise steps and purposeful contact allowing the audience to engage in the seduction of the dance. Huge lifts and gliding bodies moving in a slow passionate seduction depicting a very sexy lady entrancing her man into a powerful love story. The last note played, and as we practiced, I slid down Brian's leg and at the last moment Brian threw me back backward over his thigh letting go and allowing me to balance on my over it on my own.

The crowd erupted. Whistles, clapping, callouts! It was all so thrilling. It's been a long time since we both performed together. It has been even longer that we did this professionally with this size audience. Guard stood still, his eyes intensified and a direct gaze watching my every movement.

As we walked off stage, Becca met me with a mega hug and grabbed her guy and kissed him soundly on the mouth.

"You were both amazing. Honey, you were so hot," she declared, latching on to hubby.

We walked behind the stage to avoid the crowd. We found Guard in the parking lot. Still looking so unbelievably handsome! Wearing his black jeans, white tight t-shirt and standard always necessary badass biker boots and so hot! He scooped me into his arms and twirled be around. When he finally stopped he kissed me deeply on the mouth knocking the wind right out of me.

"Fucking beautiful, angel," he said in a husky voice.

"Thank you." I blushed and lowered my eyes.

I turned my attention back to my friends who truly really are my family and with a few teary goodbyes later, I watched them drive away. Brian tried to pacify both Becca and I reminding us that I would see them for the photo shoot on Wednesday and that made me feel a little better. Guard came up behind me and pulled me close. He kissed my neck. Then took my hand and led me back, walking past the party and led me in front of the Satan's Pride MC building.

He turns me to face him and spans my waist, gripping tight, "Ava, I want you to do something for me."

"What?" I said, tilting my head to the side.

"There's another party going on in there." He said jerking his head in the direction of Satan's Pride Headquarters. "I want you to come in with me. Before you walk in I want to prepare you for what you're going to see."

"Huh?"

"All right, angel, I am going to give you the down-and-dirty version. We have a visiting club over and when they visit we throw parties. I want you to keep close to me and never let go of my hand. You are not wearing my patch and I don't want anyone thinking you're fair game. I don't want to have to kill someone tonight." He growled the last bit.

This was him informing me of a party? Not liking this very much. Or at all.

"Patch? What?" I said confused, then decided that I should just go home. "Um... maybe I should stay here. You go to the party. I don't mind," I said and obviously I couldn't contain my nervousness.

His hand snaked around my waist and looped his finger in my jean shorts as he pulled me close. Moved his lips to my neck and kissed me softly. He continued to trace a line of kisses to my ear and whispered, "I want you with me, angel. I want you beside me. You're safe with me, I won't let go of you. I promise."

I took a breath and blew it out reminding myself that I am not a coward. "Okay," I whispered.

Still holding me close. "Before we head in, any guy who's not wearing a Satan's Pride jacket extends a hand to you, you do NOT take it. You do not take a drink from anyone but me; you do not leave my side. They say something you do not like, you do not respond." Guard was looking very severe.

I was beginning to rethink my decision. By this time I was being led to the door and then through the door.

I was two feet in the door when looked around to see most of the women wearing less than a string bikini. I took a step back and would have continued if Guard didn't have a firm grip on my hand pulled me to him. I looked at Guard and he was already sizing up my face. "Eyes on me, angel," he instructed, as he continued to pull me further inside.

I am the ice queen. I have the perfected the poker face and I was having a hard time with keeping my face free of expression. OMG! Girls giving blowjobs! Openly having sex right here in front of me, in front of everyone and threesomes! Holy shit! My heart was racing. What the hell is this? I am in hell!

I looked up at Guard's face again, eyes like steel. He stopped finally in a secluded corner of the massive warehouse that was made to look like a giant living room. Couches, tables, big-screen TV, stereo systems, pool table and that's just what I could see. There are rooms that lead off to other areas and people were moving to and from those hallways. Guard dropped into an armchair taking me with him. I was on his lap and he settled me so that I was on one knee and his other was locking me in place.

He whispered near my ear, "Angel, eyes." So I looked into his eyes. He pulled my mouth to his and kissed me slowly, taking his sweet time tasting me. I think this is his way of keeping me calm. It was actually quite effective.

The rough voice rumbled, "Guard."

"Wire."

My head jerked up as well when I heard a gruff voice. This man was dangerous. He was wearing a jacket with a different emblem, labeled Notorious Roads. A scar marked his face, over his right cheekbone. His eyes roamed my frame and made no secret about it. He looks me over and over and over. He actually licked his lips like I was dessert on the menu. With a sly sneer, Wire extended his hand out to me.

I stiffen in Guard's arms, when I hear Guard voice, "Mine." It was a fierce growl, sounding like an angry wolf ready to attack. I felt his arm band around me very tightly.

"Not willing to share? Not very friendly." Spitting the words out with sarcasm. His eyes continued to drill down on me, "We can work her together." These words slithered out and I was about to jump out of my skin. I'm sure I stopped breathing.

# Guard

"Lots to choose from, Wire, she's mine. Feel free to roam. I am sure you'll find something you like." Guard was talking through his teeth trying to keep his cool.

"I like the pretty dancer. Saw you on stage, pretty girl. Dance for me and your reward will be very generous." Wire stared and his eyes roamed over me again.

Okay, I was very close to bolting and I know Guard knew this because one hand was firmly on my waist and the other was turning my head to face him. He dipped his head to kiss me and murmured, "Eyes on me, angel." I kept my eyes on Guard and he snuggled me into his side.

"Pretty dancer belongs to *me*," he stated firmly. Then he called out for Orion. "Our guest is looking for a special someone, find him what he wants," he directed. Turning back to Wire. "Orion will take care you getting it wet. I am taking *my* pretty girl upstairs." He used Wire's word and I could see a vein bulge in his neck.

With those final parting words, Guard lifted me into his arms and I instinctively wrapped my arms around his neck to hold on. He called Demon over and when we were at the stairs he said, "No one comes near my room. Get War to stand watch."

He carried me up a set of stairs and I was too frazzled to say anything.

Once in his room I glanced around to notice it was furnished with only the basic necessities, one of which is a very large bed. He lowered me tenderly right in the middle. He sat on the edge of the bed and I knew he was waiting for me to gather myself up and look at him. I just couldn't yet. I didn't want him to see my fear. I was freaking out on the inside and didn't want to make it that apparent on the outside.

"Angel?"

"Yes," keeping me eyes on the bed.

"Look at me."

"Not yet," I replied.

"Not yet?" he chuckled.

"Nope." I very much popped the "p" in nope.

"We're going to talk," he insisted.

"Not much to say." Then I lifted my eyes. "I don't belong here." I let out a breath.

"You belong with me and I am here. You're here," he declared. That was emphatic.

I was twisting my hands in my lap. "I do not judge others. I firmly believe that each person gets to decide what they do and how they do it. I however do not fit what's going on here. I can see that this scene is normal for you. Not for me. Never for me." I said this firmly, shaking my head.

"No one here is going to make you do what you don't want to happen."

"I beg to differ. I think if you were not around Scarface or whatever his name would not have given in quite so easily. Downstairs could have ended very different," I said with a shaky voice. "Please take me home," I asked quietly.

"He eyed you on stage. Saw you dancing, got a hard-on for you. My men heard this and kept eyes on you, keeping you safe. Fucker always wants class; doesn't respect it but wants it. You were safe then and you are safe now," he insisted.

He reached out and cupped my face with his two large hands. His thumb stroked my cheek. He lowered his forehead to mine and brushed his lips against mine.

"Stay with me," he whispered against my lips. I want to shake my head but just stayed still instead.

Then he took his hands away leaving our lips touching. "Kiss me, angel. I have been waiting for you to kiss me." He wanted me to kiss him?

"We've kissed," I whispered back. Not moving and barely breathing.

"I kiss you; you never initiate kissing me." He continued. "Give me your mouth, angel."

I blinked.

He was right. And I wanted to kiss him. I loved his mouth, his lips warm and soft.

Cautiously, I touch his jaw with my fingertips, letting them linger before tracing them along his neck and finally resting them on his shoulders. I pluck up my courage and licked his lower lip and tilted my head and pressed my lips to his. He allowed me a moment of take charge and then his mouth opened and I was besieged with tongue and lips. I was being shoved back ward into the soft mattress. I moaned as I felt his weight down on me. His tongue in my mouth teasing, darting in, tasting me. His rough hands move over me. One runs a trail to my breast; even with my shirt I can feel the heat from his hand. The other hand moving to my ass. Tracing circular patterns and squeezing me, pulling me up to his body. I can feel his hard cock pushing into my midsection.

# Guard

I love the feel of his body, his mouth licking and kissing his way down. Finally reaching my breast straining again the material of my shirt, I deep moan escapes my throat.

"Fuckin' amazing," he growled.

I don't even notice he's unbuttoned the three buttons holding my shirt closed. The last button pops open and his fingers pull my bra down exposing on deep pink nipple. I sucked in a breath as Guard's mouth closed over it suckling gently at first and increasing the pull into his mouth. My back arches off the bed. Another strained moan and my hands move to his head in a silent plea to hold him there. I can feel this powerful sensation moving through me down in between my legs.

What's happening to me, I am panting and moaning, writhing beneath him. Moving his lips back to mine assaulting my mouth over and over until I simply let him take what he wants. I abandon all thought and give in to this moment.

Guard tears his mouth from mine for a split second to remove his t-shirt. His mouth on me again, he positions himself between my legs grinding his lower half against mine. My breathing hitches and I gasp.

"Fuck me, angel. I wanna hear you come for me," he moaned into my mouth.

I strained under him, moving instinctively trying to release a pressure building inside me.

Guard took my hands pushed them up to either side of my head hold them there with his hands laced through them. Leveraging his lower body so I can feel his cock straining against is jeans his continued to move and grind against me.

I want him! I need him! I need this!

"Please," I begged. My voice is husky and strained. My body arched to push against him wanting to prolong the contact as he move against me.

I ache and move trying to adjust myself under him, moving with him.

Guard takes both my hands in one of his over my head and explores my body with the other. Mouth on mine, tongue darting in and out and then little licks down to my breast cherishing them with attention of suckling. I feel the snap of my jean shorts. My breathing becomes more laboured.

His fingers slide into my shorts under my panties and find their way to my core.

A tense guttural sound finds its way out of my body. I don't even recognize it came from me.

A sudden shyness and I try to close my legs, stopped by his thighs holding me open and exposed. Guard lifts his head and looks into my eyes noticing my wariness and kisses me deeply. "Come for me, baby. I need to hear you, angel," he growled huskily.

Lost in his mouth his finger found its way into my slit. "So wet. Angel, you're so wet for me."

I moaned in his mouth as his fingers continued their assault on my clit. Slow circular motions making me buck beneath him. I mew and gasp with each touch.

"Oh, please. Baby, please," I panted. Husky moans strangling my throat.

"Give me your eyes, angel," Guard commanded.

I raised my eyes to his and he rewards me with the pressure and flick of his thumb against my nub.

Oh, God.

My legs strained and tensed as an immense shudder pierces though my body. I cry out in a low gut wrenching moan from deep inside me. I am lost in oblivion for what seems eternity before glided back to down. Guard slows his fingers and pulls his hand out of my panties, releases my hands and gathers me in his arms.

My head in the crook of his arm wrapped in his arms, I suddenly feel very vulnerable. I gain control of my laboured breathing. If I close my eyes tight thinking I can blot out what just happened. I can sense his eyes scanning me.

What is Guard thinking of me? Mind you, I heard his words of encouragement pushing me to the edge of reason.

Do I say something? Then I hear his voice.

"Angel, look at me."

"No," I said quietly.

"No?" he chuckled. He twisted his body so that we were facing each other. "Look at me, baby."

I opened my eyes to see his beautiful eyes staring back. "What's happening in that head of yours?"

I blinked but don't answer.

"Angel, let me in, baby," he said softly, caressing my cheek.

"I…I…" then I just shake my head. I couldn't formulate words. I start to close my eyes when I hear a firm voice.

# Guard

"You are not shutting down. Not in my arms and not in my bed." His voice raw and direct.

Tears formed in my eyes. I need to tell him.

"You promise me you won't tease or laugh at me?" I ask warily.

Sensing my anxiety, he nodded and moves me so that our bodies are in full contact. "Tell me, baby."

"This is the first time I never faked it," I whisper. I started to move away, but he would have none of that.

Now it was his turn to blink a few times. This is followed by a long lingering kiss, so deep, and slow. When he finally pulled back, he asked quietly, "Want to explain this now or later?"

"Later." I lowered my eyes.

"Close your eyes, baby. Sleep now," he said pulling the blanket over the both of us, holding me close.

I let my eyes close and I shut down into a blissful sleep.

# Chapter 6

## Confessions

I stretch out and collided with a rock. Except this rock is pulling me close, nuzzling my neck and shoulder.

"Mornin', angel." I hear a sexy voice. He turns me on just saying good morning.

"Morning," I said shyly. "Um, I think should get home, Guard," I began saying.

"Not yet. My sexy angel, you feel good." His hands roamed my body. Moving down my thigh and his mouth settling on a soft spot near my ear, nipping and lick and kissing.

Oh, my, I am a goner if he keeps this up. I have absolutely no resolve when it comes to Guard and that mouth.

"Guard, are you in there?" A loud gruff voice and heavy pounding at the door.

"Shit timing! Fuck, this better be worth it." He squeezes me one last time before getting out of bed. I sit up to watch him open the door and walk out into the hallway.

Got out of bed thinking this is a good time to pull myself together. I made my way to the bathroom. I looked like hell. I never sleep fully dressed and my makeup. I need a get home and have a hot shower and maybe drop back into my bed. If I bury myself in my room I won't have to face Guard and explain last night.

Thought of our night filled me. Fuck, he turned me on. I have never ex-perienced an orgasm. I'm thirty-five years old and was married for five years and never experience an explosion like last night. A heat came over my entire body just recalling what he made me feel last night.

I washed my face, loving the cool refreshing water splashing my face. I pulled my fingers through my hair and created a messy ponytail tying it back with an elastic I had in my purse.

I feel a little better. I step back out into the bedroom seeing that Guard has not come back yet. I still hear voices outside the bedroom door.

"Where's War? I want him to take Ava home. I want her out of here before the meeting starts and before Wire gets an idea where to find her. He freaked her out last night and was pretty pissed I refused him. War stays with her until I get there. I want him on his game," he said.

"Jesus, you think he's that stupid? That's whacked that he starts shit over a woman." I recognized the name to be Orion.

"This is the first woman I claimed in Satan's Pride and she's mine. Wire is looking to cause shit so I want Ava under watch until he is out of town," Guard said.

What? Claimed? Wire's pissed?

Oh, shit!

"Is Vi still here?" Guard asked.

"Yeah, why?" Orion asked.

"Wire latch to her?" he asked.

"No fuckin' way that shit is happening!" Orion declared.

"You soundin' jealous, Orion. Get her out of here too." He persisted in teasing. "Keep talkin' like that and I think we have two serious women in Satan's Pride."

"Fuck off!" I could hear a few clops of feet. "I'm going to get War." I can hear the thick sounds of footsteps making their way down the hall.

A door opens to a shirtless Guard.

Oh, my!

Chiseled abs, thick shoulders, massive biceps and the sexiest pattern of tattoos interwoven on his olive skin. He makes me winded. I tear my gaze away from him. I scan around the room for my shoes, giving me some other to do than stare at an Adonis. I don't remember taking them off last night but they're not on my feet so they must be somewhere in this room.

"Looking for something?" he teased, arms crossed standing two feet away as I'm bending to check under the bed.

"Shoes," I mumbled, continuing my search in a desperate effort not to make eye contact. "Angel, over here."

"I need my shoes." Maybe I can buy myself more time before I need to look at that smoldering man again.

"Baby. Right. Here. Now." I could tell he was getting impatient, each word was accentuated.

I stood up and looked at him. My shoes hanging from his fingers. I extend my hands, holding them out ready to take them.

"Thank you," I said, not looking at him but looking at my shoes.

He didn't extend my shoes but jerked my hand towards him and found myself plastered against the wall of his chest. Guard drops my shoes to the floor and I have hands flat against his chest, I looked up at him bewildered, "We still have a talk to get through." Before I could even reply he went on to say, "Not now. I am having War take you home. Get some coffee in you and I will be by later."

"You have lots to do; we can do it another time." I didn't look up and kept my eyes on my hands.

"I want your eyes and this is the last time I am going to say this." He waits for my eyes to reach his. He was getting annoyed. He pulls both arms around me like a vice. He backs himself into a love seat hauling me with him, making this so that I am straddling his lap. Arms locked tight around me like steel.

"Ava, I run a decent club. We protect this town and we run decent businesses. Not always been like this and the rival MC's look for a way to bring their shit onto our club. I gotta deal with their shit today. I wanna know that when I'm done I get to come see you and have your mouth on mine. You owe me words and we decide how we make us fit. I am not letting you go. You belong to me. I knew this when I saw you clicking heels in the parking lot. Sunglasses covered your eyes but I knew you felt it," he explained.

"I felt you," I said. No point in lying, he would see through that. My handing gripping his shoulders to support myself and hold steady as his words were making me dizzy. "This scares me. That man yesterday scares me. I am not those women down there. I'm just not and I don't want to be. Ever!"

"I'm here and I'll protect you and this. You gotta give a little and get that I will have your back. You gotta have mine. Can't let you go. Won't let you go.

You gotta come to terms and accept this." He laid it out. No wavering, just sheer determination.

I sucked in a breath of air. He wants to protect me. Sounds so nice. I don't know what to say to I just stay quiet and look at him.

"War is taking you home. I'll be by later. I cook for you, we'll talk. Now kiss me so I can go take care of shit."

"I have to go get groceries," I said, my hands now moving down his arms.

"I got it. Go home, relax. I'll be there soon." He moved one large hand to the back of my head and draws me in for a long, sweet kiss. I wrap my arms around his neck and press close. I little sigh leaves my mouth as he moves back.

He moves me to stand, hands me my shoes and once fastened he leads me to the back entrance of the Satan's Pride complex and tucks me into the passenger side of a Jeep. Rambling off instructions to War in what seems a totally different language, a quick solid kiss on the mouth and the door shuts.

"Be good, baby." He winked.

War would make a terrible babysitter. Definitely not a talker and certainly not loose-lipped. Guard would be so proud. He would rival the guards at the British palace in not making a sound or move.

I have a bodyguard. I sit outside, he sits outside. I move to the kitchen he moves to the kitchen. No words, though, that would be too personal.

Sheesh! I was a people person and I had no idea how to communicate with this man.

"How about some lunch?" I asked sweetly.

"Sure," he said.

"You like pasta?" Again I was adjusting my tone to be candy-like.

"Sure."

"Want some garlic bread with that?" I was looking at the fridge and going through the left over from the other night. Now I was just going for a different word than "sure."

"Sure." Well, at least he was consistent.

I warmed up pasta and garlic bread for War. I made myself a salad. He refused a beer, only by gesture, I never heard the word no, so I told him to help himself to whatever was there.

After clearing the dishes, I gave up on a two way conversation and I told him I was going upstairs and he was welcome to watch TV. He nodded and up I went. Truly one of the oddest non-conversations I had.

# Guard

After a hot shower I threw on a pair of baby blue yoga shorts and white tank. I decided make some coffee. I handed a cup to War and walked back upstairs and sat on my terrace on my lounge. I stared out to the lake.

I have coffee. I have my lake. I close my eyes feeling the warm breeze drift across my face. Thoughts of Guard invade my mind. His face, his lips, his strong arms, and even his possessive nature bring back vivid memories of previous evening.

"Where are you, angel?" Guard's smooth voice asked.

He is standing just inside the door leading out to the bedroom terrace. My eyes open, and I turn my head. My heart stops. He is so hot. Jeans and t-shirt, his typical uniform works for him. His wavy dark hair is blowing in the breeze. He takes my breath away.

"Hi." I smiled. "How was your meeting?"

"Too fucking long." He strolled to the lounge I was sitting on, edging me forward and sliding in behind me. One arm holding tight at my waist the other moving the strap of my tank and replacing it with his lips and tongue.

I moved to give him more access. Mmm, that feels so good. I dropped my head back to his shoulder and turned my head. I wanted his mouth on mine. I kissed his lips then slid my tongue into his mouth tentatively. Guard kissed me back deepening our kiss, holding my head steady with is hand in my hair. So sweet, so soft and sexy, I am done for.

I'm in trouble.

He pulled away and our head tilting to touch one another.

"Yeah, angel, love your mouth. Baby, I am trying to go slow with you. I know last night was a shock. I am proud of how you saw it through," all the while kissing my neck. "Baby, I want to fuck you. I want to bury myself so deep inside you that all I can feel is your pussy wet and slick. But before I do, angel, I want to have our talk."

I slide off the lounge and take his hand and pull for him to get up. I lead him back into the bedroom. Silently I lead him to the bed. "Sit, please."

I take run my fingers through my hair, and pace back and forth. Where do I start? He's going to think I'm a freak. Then like a damn bursting I erupted into my life story.

Guard watches me pace back and forth. I could tell he was holding in the urge to push the conversation along.

"I met James when I was twenty-three years old. He was a good man and he was funny and kind. I fell in love with him and he adored me. He took his time with me. We made out, fooled around it fun." I kept pacing. "James never pushed me into sex. He said he wanted it to be perfect and special. I thought he was sweet and romantic. I never thought any more about it. Then, he proposed after two years later and that was the first night we slept together. The night we got engaged, he wanted everything to be perfect." I stopped for a second and looked at Guard making firm eye contact. "It was lovely and sweet and I figured since it was my first time that was it." I shrugged my shoulder and kept going. "I was fine with that. James kept trying to make it more because he knew I didn't or couldn't climax. I knew it was bothering him that he could and I couldn't, get there." I was wringing my hands together at this point, my anxiety was growing. "I started worrying about him and I because he was constantly trying to make it better and was making it worse. I got to thinking that there is something wrong with me and I went to visit my doctor. She told me to relax and let it come naturally. James wouldn't relax! It was like an obsession. I couldn't take the pressure, so I started faking it." I breathed out heavily.

I took a second, and went on. "He calmed down. I liked everything else we did so I figured so what if I didn't climax. We were happy in every other way. I was married to a great guy and our lives continued as always. We were happy! He supported and encouraged me in all I did. The modelling, the dancing, the band, my friends, he was great with all we had. I didn't want to lose a great man because I was broken. It was my fault and he was so sensitive I didn't want him to think it was him."

I ended with, "Then last night I have no idea what happened and it all freaked me out." I finally stopped talking. My hands were shaking. I looked at him and wait for him to call me crazy and walk out.

"Come here, baby." He held his hand out.

I took it hesitantly and he led me to him. He pulled in onto the bed and centered me with my head on the pillows and his leg spreading mine open and settling between them. Very intimate. My arms braced at his shoulders; his hand directing my face to his. "I think you have some catching up to do, angel." His voice was a low growl.

Really! I blink.

My heart skips a beat and my eyes widen. "War, is down…" I start.

"Gone, angel. Left when I got here." And his fingers started moving under my tank top, easing it upward, pulling it off completely. He continues talking as his hands move across my skin ever so gently; little flutters across my body. "This is how it's gonna go, baby. Today and tonight is about getting my angel to moan pretty and beg me for more. It's all about you, baby, and making you come until you are so exhausted that you fall asleep in my arms."

I am speechless. The thought of him on me and in me was making me crazy. I don't do this, I don't feel this. I can't. My breath is coming in short pants. My breasts are straining against the material of my cotton bra. My cheeks turn pink with embarrassment; I can feel how wet I am getting and he has barely touched me yet.

He was admiring my simple white bra with a delicate tiny daisy in the centre. A sly smile moves across his lips kissing the skin above the daisy and removes it. I can't breathe! His lips feel so good.

He lips move along the curve of my breast along with his hands. One hand cups my breast while the other is lavished with butterfly kisses, which turn into little licks. At which point I can't control a soft moan rising through me.

I can feel his lips on my nipple, suckling gently, while his other hand gently pulls and rolls my nipple as I squirm beneath him.

He continues his assault by giving the same attention to each breast. I arch my back giving him all access, straining closer.

"Hush, angel. Nice and slow. I want this nice and slow," he rumbled moving his lips down my stomach across my hips. Hands pulling down my shorts, easing them over my hips and ass. Doing the same with my panties until I was completely bare. I was feeling a little self-conscious being completely naked while Guard was still fully dressed. I made a move to cover myself and that was instantly stopped with a look that held me firm.

Guard disentangles himself from my arms, moving back onto look at full at the length of me. I want to feel him on me. I move to reach out and touch him and he stops my holding my wrist.

"I. Touch. You. Stay still for me, angel. No touching me. Stay perfectly still."

Oh, God, is he kidding!

I nodded, hesitantly.

He placed his hands on either side of my head and kissed my brow, cheeks, jaw, chin, lips with feather light kisses. His hands never touching me. He moves lower to my neck, collarbone, giving bountiful attention to my breasts. Then moving lower still with nothing but his lips and finding hidden soft spots along the way making me moan and beg for more. He stops right above my core and changes direction.

I see him reach for my left leg, lifts it and moves to suck and lick my toes. My body jolts with the new pleasure. I cried out and although Guard is looking into my eyes, his lips continue to move up my leg, knee, and inner thigh and begins the assault on my right leg.

I can feel the tension building inside me. Each kiss, his breath against my body. My fists holding tight into the comforter to ground me.

After having kissed me all over, I can feel his breath between my legs. "You're so wet for me, angel. I am gonna to eat you, baby, for a long, long time." He stretched out those words in a low deep growl. Separating my slit with one think long finger, I then feel his tongue lap over the entire length of my pussy.

My body jolts.

My back arches off the bed.

A definite primal moan escapes my throat. My breasts heave, unable to control my breathing. Guard's hands were holding me firm, another long lick and then he blew softly a cool breath on my clit creating an intense shudder from my chest to my thighs.

He sucked hard on my clit. I felt his hands on my ass holding me still. His mouth deep, his tongue circling my clit and then he sucks the whole nub into his mouth. I can't breathe. He licked and nibbled and sucked until I cried out and let go. My body shudders and waves upon waves ripples through my body.

My eyes closed in I feel my body slowly descending from the out-of-body experience.

I am exhausted. I can't feel my legs. I don't think I can move.

But Guard is not done with me. His fingers still moving on my pussy; he moves up my body keeping his hand occupied between my legs. A long sweet kiss as I still try and get my breathing in check. Guard whispers, "Not done yet, baby. I want to hear more."

"I don't think I can," I said. I didn't know my own body because my face was already lighting up for him. My legs were widened as his touch continued and my nipples ached for his touch.

"I know you can, angel. Feel my fingers." And with that he plunged to fingers deep inside me making my breath hitch and a growl emerge from deep inside. He was relentless in is attack. "Ride my fingers, angel." He commanded. "Move with me, baby."

I was desperate to ease the building pressure inside me so I did as I was told. With his mouth on my breasts and fingers creating magic inside me, it wasn't long before I exploded in his arms. My body was taunt and I peaked once more.

He wrapped his arms around me. Lying on his side with his legs ensnaring me. He was looking down on me; one hand propped to support his body and the other in my hair. Guard tugged my hair forcing my eyes to me his. His kisses are gentle, sweet.

"You came hard for me, angel. How do you feel?" he whispered.

"Um...good," I whispered back and tried to shut my eyes to stop him from seeing my embarrassment. Guard wouldn't have it.

"No, baby, eyes on me." Making sure that we were nose to nose, eyes direct he said, "Hands down seeing you on fire at my touch was the most perfect thing I ever saw. You are so beautiful and to know that I am the only one that can get you there makes me fuckin' wild. I want this night to be yours but very soon I am going to take you and fuck you so that I can see your wild eyes with me inside you."

Guard finished with, "Never hide this from me. I want to see you on fire for me." He held me close. So sweet.

Kind and gentle.

He is sexy, and thoughtful. I can't get him out of my mind. Even the first encounter at the grocery store and I could feel his presence.

No, I can't make this more. Just take this day for what it is. I don't even know his real name.

Oh, crap, how to have feelings for someone without knowing their name?

"Guard?" I asked quietly.

"Yeah, baby."

"Will you tell me your real name?" I asked shyly.

He nuzzled his nose to mine. Kissed my lips and said, "Gabriel Stone."

I smiled at him. "Thank you for telling me, honey."

"Yeah, angel." His face and voice goes very soft.

I revelled in the thought that I am sure that this is not common knowledge and he trusted me with it.

It was a long while later when we made our way downstairs and made dinner together. We ate, drank wine, kissed and Gabriel "Guard" Stone showed me ecstasy three more times that night without ever giving me his cock but promising that I would share that with him very soon. We fell asleep naked in my bed. I was utterly and completely happy and satisfied. The first night I have ever slept all the way through.

# Chapter 7
# Guard's Release

T he beginning of a new week. I wake to find an empty place next to me replaced by my cell phone. I see the text light flashing.

"Good mornin', angel. Loved tasting you last night. The crew and I have some work to do out of town. Friday night you're mine. Prepare, baby."

I respond, "Morning, honey. Have a productive meeting. I have my photo shoot Wednesday. Client wants display ads ASAP. Miss you."

Do I hit send? I do miss him. Why shouldn't I tell him? I bite my lip and remind myself that I am not a coward. I hit send.

Guard wrote, "Miss you too, baby."

A tiny squeal and those four little words. I was grinning huge.

I jumped in the shower and put it text out of my head. I was going to check emails and get into town for Milly's amazing coffee.

It was a great trip to town. I met up with Vi at the diner and we talked about Satan's Pride, filling me in on some details. There are fifty members, not all in town at one time unless there is a major function. Guard is the president and Orion is his right hand. Demon is the main muscle and War is the newest up the rank. Rig and Bang have been away working with ally clubs on the expansion of the parts manufacturing but they were part of the original crew.

This club is a brotherhood. They are a young club and at thirty-seven years of age, Guard was the oldest and most experienced. He started at seventeen and was asked to start something out this way from his original brothers. They are still tight and work together but Guard built this. He did them proud.

All the women at that party were strippers and prostitutes, except Vi and I. They never come to town unless they are hosting a party. Guard tells his men to go get want they want but to leave the town clean. Vi also explained that Orion and she are seeing one another but Orion hasn't given her his patch yet. He calls her his "old lady" but still hasn't sealed it with a ring or patch. An ugly word for partner in my opinion but Vi thinks it's cute.

I took it all in and asked her, "Why do you stick around if he won't commit to you?"

"There is no leaving the club, Ava, once I accept, he is mine and I am his. I want this but Orion has had some bad relationships and he is being cautious," she explained. "Orion said that Guard has claimed you, Ava. He won't let you go. How are you doing with that?"

I must have blushed deeply.

"Ava, you like him a lot!" she giggled.

I never directly answered Vi but we she knew I was falling in love with Gabriel "Guard" Stone. I have been in this town for a month and my life was filling with happy.

Every morning and every night Guard and I exchanged texts. Some sweet words and others that made me blush. I am thirty-five and have never sexted. Those tests were from Guard.

I reminded Guard that I was in New York with Brian and Becca. He called me the night before so that we could hear one another. It wasn't a long chat but I liked how he called me angel.

It was good to be with Brian and Becca for a couple of days. I was able to make some great meals and stick them in the freezer for Becca. I was thinking that she could rest as she was getting bigger, more tired and cranky. Highly volatile and emotional without being pregnant she was all over the place now. I kind of felt bad for Brian. He's a trooper! Makes his wife feel like no one else exists.

The photo shoot took eight hours. They were wanting for five major pictures to hang in their stores for a new line, catering to the edgy crowd. I almost died laughing when I saw the Harley in the studio. The clothes were cool. The boots did produce a "come fuck me" vibe but in a sexy, classy, elegant way.

Brian had tracks of music he knew I would turn me into the character he wanted in his shots. He knows how I leave myself and just float into being someone else. Hours of posing and we finally have the five perfect pictures. We had thousands of pictures! He showed me the "perfect" five and I was pretty pleased.

One was a one-piece bathing suit in leather with a lace cover-up threaded through my hands creating a sexy shear. The second was dark blue jeans, sexy red Harley t-shirt and matching jacket. The killer pose was when I was lying across the bike with legs on the handles; body pulled tight and head on the seat. The third was me in torn light blue jeans, white tank top, grease on my fingers and smeared on my cheek, with a rag in one hand and a wrench in the other. It was fun and playful. The fourth was a red sexy dress, high kick-ass biker boots with a sense of come get me.

It was the last one that had Brian stoked. I was belly down on the seat of the bike, wild hair, soft morning makeup, the pose was soft. My lips were slightly open, my eyes lowered, my hands lightly on the bike. It was hard meets soft. Brian loved it and I thought it was pretty good.

I came, I posed and now I was anxious to get home to my place and to Guard.

*Friday Morning*
Guard sends a text, "Angel, meet me in town this afternoon."

"Okay, honey. Where?"

"There's a parts store beside Satan's Pride. Picking up and will take you to dinner. 4 P.M."

"See you then."

I was going to see Guard again. My heart did a little happy dance. Last time I saw him he made orgasm over and over again. I look in the mirror and still blush at way he made my body cry out in rapture from the onslaught of his mouth, tongue and hands.

I decided a cute summer dress with in pale yellow with spaghetti straps, just above the knee. I matched them with strappy high heel white sandals and simple pearl earrings. I left my hair loose letting it hang below the shoulders blades. I kept my makeup natural and fresh. Topped my lips with pale pink gloss and head out to see my guy. I came to the conclusion that if he kept calling me his that I could call him mine.

I made my way into town and into the main strip. It took me a few minutes to find the shop Guard was talking about because the door was covered by

Satan's Pride jackets. Now I think that should have been the first clue that I was in the right spot.

I have to get past at least twenty biker bad asses lining the store.

"Excuse me," I asked quietly, tapping the first guy on the arm.

He took a quick look at me at stepped aside. It was like the parting of the red sea, and each biker moved either to the left or right allowing me to get by. It was freaky!

Freakier was the way they were staring at me as I made it inside the store. I looked back a couple of times as I to notice some smirks and raised eyebrows. I see War, and Demon they were definitely smirking.

I see Orion. "Hey, is Guard here?"

"Oh, yeah. He's here! He's right over there."

Orion points towards the wall at the far end of the room. A little hint of teasing in that tone he was using. A little unnerving is what I am getting from all this.

I start walking towards Guard and he must have heard my heels clinking on the floor. He turned sharply, hands on hips with a look on his face I couldn't read. I slowed my pace mainly because I was trying to read his expression and a little because he looked fierce.

His gaze went to the wall and then back to me. I looked over at the wall too. That's when I stopped dead.

Oh. My. God.

There were pictures of me in huge poster form in frames lined up along the wall. Not just any pictures but the pictures Brian took just a few days ago. I looked at the pictures and then at Guard and then back at the pictures.

Was he angry? He knew I modelled. What's he freaking out about?

He started to walk slowly towards me. I however was backing up. FAST.

"Ava! Where are you going?" he asked in a low growl.

"Um, Guard. Are you mad?" I asked cautiously, still backing up.

"Why would I be mad, angel?" he said in that same menacing tone. He was still moving towards me with purpose.

"I don't know." I shrugged. "You shouldn't be. You knew I modelled." Yet I kept stepping back as he stepped forward.

"Angel, do you know where these are distributed?" again in the husky growl.

"No. Why would it matter?" I sounded confused and shaking my head.

"Every mechanic and parts place that carry that brand. And that's everywhere, Ava!" he shouted.

Oh, no!

Well, now I was backing up faster trying to place a little more distance between us. "Guard, those pictures are nice. The clothing covered all essential places and I made sure of it when I picked them."

"Stop moving, Ava! There is nowhere to go," he commanded.

I stopped and saw we were putting on a show for the crew of dudes hanging in the shop. There were full blown smirks and laughter bellowing around the room.

Now I was getting a little peeved. I have nothing to be ashamed of. What right does he have to be pissed off? That's it, I am having my say.

"All right, now I'm pissed!" I emphasized this by stomping my foot. Guard's eyebrow quirked upward and held fast his position.

"Are you now?" he said with attitude. I can see the glint in his eye and he placed those hands back on his hips.

"I didn't do anything wrong. Those pictures are nice and it took us hours and hours to get those shots. I didn't know how they were going to use them and that's why I take such care in making sure I'm covered." Then I admitted, "Okay, the bathing suit one is a little more revealing but it's a bathing suit. I refused the bikini! And it's how I have been making a living along with dancing for my entire life, way before you came into it. So get over it!"

So get over it? Did I actually say that? Yikes!

Oh, shit! I can see the nostrils flaring. I turned to run, but he was right on me I got has far as the counter before I was hauled into him with a giant oomph! All of sudden I found my back to his front and his arms braced tightly around my waist.

"Get over it!" he growled loudly, repeating my words. I closed my eyes when he said it; and re-opened them quickly when he jerked me even closer. I looked up and saw a bunch of very entertained bikers. They are going to be no help at all, this I was told. Brothers stick together! "Can we talk about this calmly?" I asked sweetly, thinking I should try another tactic.

"Ava, what are you thinking about to get those expressions in the pictures?" His voice was menacingly calm and smooth.

"What do you mean?" I asked confused.

"Those eyes and mouth on display like that. What are you thinking in those pictures?" he demanded.

I squirmed in his armed to turn and face him. He allowed that but make no bones about it I was tied tightly to him.

"Huh?" I was confused. "I am not thinking anything. Brian plays music into my earphones and I get lost in the music and flow he finds his moment and finds his shot. When he sees what he wants he pipes it into the room and shoots like a crazy man until he gets his perfect pose. That's how he and I work. This is how it's been for eons."

"Music? Music created that?" He points to the pictures. Guard was dumbfounded.

"Well, yeah. What else would do that?" I was still very confused. "I have been surround by music my entire life. You see me dance you know I move as I feel. You do know this, right?" I said sarcastically.

He slackened his hold and looked into my face. "Fuck me." He stares as me for what seems like eternity.

"Are you still mad?" I asked tentatively.

His response was swinging me up in his arms and started to walk towards the door, while I shrieked. "What are you doing? Where are we going? Guard, put me down. Damn it. Put. Me. Down!"

"Angel! Quiet! Stay still, woman!" he growled loudly. He then lowered his voice and quietly said in my ear, "I have only so much self-control and I am a notch away from not caring who is around when I fuck you."

I immediately stopped squirming, looked into his face then nuzzled into his neck.

"Okay, honey."

# Chapter 8
## Gabriel's Passion

Guard carried me off, and I was expecting him to toss me in the air to land in his bed; half expected him start tearing at my clothes. I was anticipating that his temperament has shortened his patience.

I was very, very wrong.

Guard carried me to the sofa and kept on his lap. I unclenched my hands from around his neck and pressed against his chest and whispered. "Gabriel," I called him his given name because what we were going to do was extremely personal and passionate to me.

His lips met mine and he kissed me wholly and deeply.

He was surprisingly gentle and sweet. It was soft and slow, building the anticipation of what will follow.

I felt his tongue probe my mouth and my mouth mimicked his. Our tongues dueling and our need become more hurried. He was showing great restraint. His hands flowed over my body.

He broke our kisses. "Need to have you. I need to be in you deep, angel."

And I shivered as I could feel his need for me, for us.

"Yes," I muttered against his mouth. I was panting with need too.

He moved to lift and carry me to his bed. Placing me gently in the centre of the bed and backed away to take of his t-shirt. All I could do was watch. He was perfect. His body was strong, chiselled and firm. He took off his boots, leaving him standing in his jeans.

Oh, my! I wanted to touch him. He must have sensed my need as his knee hit the bed and laid me back so that my back hit the soft mattress.

His eyes met mine as his hands went to my wrists at his chest. He moved one down, to the hard bulge in his jeans and I let my hand explore. I pressed my hand harder as his cock and was rewarded with a deep moan from my man. I let my other hands drift over his muscular body and curve around his back, slowly moving my hands up to explore all of him. All the while his lips roamed my neck and traced a path back to my mouth, gliding across my cheek and jaw. He was nipping at my earlobe and tantalizing the skin behind my ear.

He felt so unbelievably good I involuntarily made a noise in the back of my throat that had Guard grip my hips tight.

Guard swept his hand across my breast. I instinctively moved to press myself tighter into Guards touch. Moving his hand down to span my back, he pulled the zipper down allowing my dress to fall open. His hands continued to remove the straps from my shoulders, and kissing me gently and teasing my skin wherever he touched. He removed my dress leaving me in tiny white lace panties and my heels.

Then his hand glided up my side, inward and over my breast and, immediately, his thumb swept hard against my tight nipple. I liked that a lot. So much, my body arched and I moaned in his mouth. Guard rolled taking me with him. I was now straddling him with his long, powerful body under mine. He pulled me down hard, jeans grinding into my core. My head fell back at the deep thrust and even through his jeans I could feel the long hard length of him.

My hands moved on his chest, his ribs, his belly, and his sides as my lips moved along his rough jaw, his neck, his throat, and down. Everywhere I touched and tasted. I felt his muscles constricting. I loved the way his arm tightened and the powerful growl as his took onc hand at fisted it lightly in my hair pulling me down to his mouth and penetrating with passion. I loved it all, and I loved him.

I found myself rolled onto my back. I felt the emptiness and coolness between us as he stepped away to take off his jeans. I was entranced by his beauty. Then I noticed a piercing right there and I was shocked. I blinked and he winked at me deviously. I couldn't pull my eyes away from his beautiful length. I couldn't catch my breath.

His hands slid to my hips and hooked his fingers into my panties and tugged until I was completely bare. His fingers moved up my legs and thighs, soft as a feather.

Oh, my! I turned my face to hide my desire into the pillow.

"Angel, eyes on me, baby. I want to see all of you. You come with me inside you and eyes on me," Guard said roughly in a husky voice.

His fingers travelled down my body until they found their destination. I was so wet for him. The lightest of touch and I bucked off the bed. He loved that! I heard his growl as he attached himself to my mouth and he continued to assault my tender folds.

I whimpered as both my hands slid into his hair. As he worked my clit, his other hand rolled and tweaked my nipple. I gasped as he slid a finger inside me. My body involuntarily gripped it tight and moaned deeply.

"Yeah, baby, you're ready for me. So wet for me." But he continued and slid another finger inside, stroking and penetrating until I cried his name.

"Gabriel, please. Honey, I need you," I begged.

My body was begging for release and I wanted to him feel inside me. Guard cocked my knees and splayed my legs further apart. He settled his weight on top of me.

I could hear the ripping of a foil packet. "Ready, angel?" He breathed heavily into my ear. "Last chance. I won't be able to stop once I'm inside you."

Mouth parted and wild eyes, nipples erect and begging and my pussy so wet for him. I wanted him so badly to be inside me.

"Please," I said with a strained voice. My arms clinging to his forearms urging him forward.

"Nice and slow, angel. I want you to feel me inside you. I want you to re-member how I feel sliding into you," he murmured in my ear as he pushed the large tip of his erection inside me.

His piercing hit my clit sending this intense sensation. I thought I was coming undone. He was barely halfway inside when he slowing pulled back out and then in again. The sensation of the piercing was causing havoc with my senses.

A moan left my lips. He was showing great restraint. He clenched his teeth and continued at this agonizingly slow pace. I could feel every part of his cock expand and fill me. I wanted more. I wanted faster. I move my hips to meet him as he ground deep in me.

"Gabriel, please, more," I said breathless.

He started to thrust harder with a reckless thunder. My thrusts meeting his hard and fast, stroke for stroke. "God, you feel good, baby," Guard whispered harshly against my ear and I would have loved to return the compliment, but I lost the ability to speak.

I did however moan, which he seemed to really enjoy. I was there. I was ready to explode. I tore my mouth away from his, and was looking directly into his eyes when I lost all control. He continued to pump in and out of me until I came and when I did, I called his name with a ragged voice and riveted tightly to him.

I was still coming down from my orgasm when I felt it build again. How is this possible? Surely I couldn't. I wrapped legs around his hips.

"Baby, you gotta come again now," I heard him growl.

I was reaching and frustrated that I was so close, then felt a hand come down over my clit and press and flick my nub. We both erupt, our bodies shuddering, then turning heavy and holding each other tight. He came with his face buried in my neck his voice harsh and sexy and dominating.

Guard rolled off and kissed me. "Be right back." He disappeared into the bathroom and came out minutes later to lie beside me, tucking me close and stoking my body lightly.

I couldn't move or speak. I let him cover us both and nestled into him and let my eyes drift closed. I know that he didn't fuck me tonight; he made love to me passionately. A satisfied smile flits across my lips and sleep closed in.

I have no idea how long I slept, a warm feeling between my legs. Whiskers were tickling my thighs. And there are kisses fleeting across my hip to breast and back again where their lips started. A tremor runs through me. My eyes open in a sleepy haze.

I look down to find Guard provoking my senses with kisses. Mmm, that feels really good. He climbs further up my body pinning me down. Holding my head very still he nips and licks the column of my throat, neck, collar bone before saying roughly in my neck, "Time to get dirty, baby. Now I want to fuck you hard."

Dirty? My eyes widen, I am totally turned on.

With those words, felt myself go wet down below and my nipples harden against his chest. He impaled himself deep inside me and began fucking me hard. He wrapped my legs around his hips and commanded, "Don't let go."

# Guard

My hands curve round his back and my hips move to meet him, my mouth on his urging and coaxing him to move harder.

And then I came, so hard my head snapped back, ripping our lips apart and my back arched off the bed. His hips continued pounding, fucking me hard. I can feel the pressure building again and I strained to take more of him deeper.

"More, please." I had my nails dug into his back and my teeth in his shoulder as the continual thrusts pounded inside me. He buried himself to the hilt and I hit euphoria at the same time as Guard. His cries matched mine and our bodies jolted in unison.

It was the most spectacular moment I have ever felt. Guard kissed me softly, and untangled our bodies, rolling me to lay on him. My head on his chest, he stroked my hair, and his other hand moved lazily down my back.

"You good, angel?" he asked.

I kissed his chest. "Never better."

"I think my angel likes getting dirty," he teased. Then he lifted me further up his body and had our eyes meet.

"I want this every night. I want you naked in my bed, legs open ready for me to fuck you."

This was definitely not a question. He was serious and his eyes held firm.

"Um, I can't be here every night. I have my home and dance classes start next week." I prattled and was interrupted.

"Then I come to you," he growled.

Guard's hands moved to my ass and started a kneading and grinding his growing cock into my pussy. He was done talking and starting fucking me all over again.

I loved it.

# Chapter 9
# The Real Guard

Completely exhausted and fully sated lying in bed with my sexy biker badass lover talking about Gabriel story. He wanted me to know about the little Gabriel and how he turned into Guard.

I am humbled that he was ready to share that with me. I mean something to him.

Guard starts with, "Angel, I have a dark past. I don't know my father and my mother was an addict. I grew up in foster care where I was smacked around quite a bit from the time I was four until I left. One day when I was sixteen the foster father I was staying with came at me with a tire iron. He came at me because he wanted to know how much I could take. No other reason. I fucking lost it." His voice was low and quiet and his jaw tensed as he talked. "I ran right at him and knocked him down and started beating on him. Fist after fist, I just kept at him. I didn't know what made me stop but I did. When I got control of myself, I packed what little I had and left. I never looked back." Guard was looking intently at me searching for a reaction.

I just held him tight and said, "Go on, honey."

He placed a kiss on my forehead and went on. "I was lucky enough to meet a bunch of bikers from Red Maniacs MC. They let me ride with them. I worked for them until I could afford my own bike and took me in. They taught me about mechanics, bikes, and parts. They paid to send me to school to get my certifications as a mechanic. They are my brothers. No one treated me as good as them. I owe them." He stroked my hair and I placed my head on his heart.

"A few years back they asked me to branch out and take some of the newer members with me. We settled here and made this place our home. We stay clean for the most part. We are working through the rival MC's in the area to make a truce that we can all live with. Wire is a pain in our ass. He wants to stick with the old ways and transport shit across our lines. He runs a strip club which is fine but selling drugs out of it ain't cool with me and especially not if you want to go through our club."

He sighed. "You ready to run yet, angel?"

"Nope. I am so glad you found your brothers, honey." I then asked, "When did Gabriel become Guard?" I asked looking up at him. He moved me so that I was straddling his thighs, half lying on his chest.

"When you get patched into the club, you get a road name. They called me Guard because I was always ready to protect my brothers. They protected me when I couldn't and now I protect them." His voice was strong and husky. He was proud and strong. I loved that about him.

"You know Gabriel was the guardian angel just like you," I whispered against his chest as I kissed it lightly.

He laughed roughly his body shaking. "I don't think anyone would ever call me an angel, baby."

"You're my dark angel, honey. You showed me that I wasn't broken. Thank you, baby." I looked into his steel-blue eyes. I meant every word. I let my lips glide gently over his.

"Fuck me, angel. How did I get so lucky? What did I do to deserve this heaven?" Then he answered his own question. "I don't know and I am not questioning it. Just know that I want this. I won't let you go and I can't let you go." His voice meaningful and deep, shaking me to my very core.

He held me close and I nuzzled his neck. I loved the way he tasted. So I tasted his neck, throat and jaw. "Honey, I think we need to get dirty again," I whispered in his ear.

I can feel his lips curve upward in my hair, he was smiling. He turned his head and lifted my chin so that our lips meet for a deep, sensual, full kiss. Our tongues intermingling, he positioned me hovering over his erection. Sliding his cock back and forth lightly, his piercing move along my sensitive slit.

# Guard

He guided me down over his straining erection. Grasping my hips he pulled me down over his slick, smooth cock. I don't know when or how he had the time to put on the condom but was so glad he was ready.

"Ride me, angel."

Feeling a little uncertain, I let Guard guide me down over him and arching back up, thrusting harder and with a dedicated rhythm. I squeezed him tight trying to control my own need. It didn't take long for my damn to burst wide open and I arched back, letting my hair graze his thighs, pursuing my hard thrusts until I hear Guard's primal cry and release.

I am thrilled that I can get that sound to emit from Guard.

# Chapter 10
# Rules to Live By

Two weeks later, I was sipping coffee and tasting Milly's new coffee cake with Vi. It was good to have someone that I could talk to again. I call Brian and Becca once a week but at this stage I know that the baby brain is in full swing. I made arrangements to visit as soon as the baby is born so that I could hold pure beauty in its most innocent form.

Guard and I were settling into a sweet routine where we spent most nights together. Some nights were later than others, depending on the dance classes or the meeting from the club. First one home had the duty of starting dinner! We would watch movies, snuggle, make love and wake up in one another's arms.

Vi and I talked about what had haunted me about that party I went to with Guard. I told her about Wire freaking me out. Vi was very informative about biker code and ethics. She was schooled by Orion.

Rules as explained to me:

1.  Don't leave your man at the party unless it's with another old lady (still hate the terminology).
2.  Wearing a Biker's patch means you belong to him and all the rest you leave alone (still feeling a little "owned").
3.  Two kinds of women: serious girlfriends or sweetbutts (women who are there for sex only with the hopes that one biker dude takes a liking to her and claims her).

4. Being claimed is a biker's right to a woman he has a fancy for. (Doesn't she have a choice?)
5. Never cross your MC. (Well, duh!)
6. Never make a scene with your man in front of the other crew. (Apparently this makes for a very angry biker, and he loses credibility.)

These were the ones highlighted but I had a sneaking suspicion that there were more I was going to fall into. I asked Vi about her relationship with Orion.

"What is going on between the two of you?" I asked.

"He is kind and sweet but complicated and he only gives so much and then shuts down. Kinda like he is trying to separate me from another part of him."

I could tell she was trying to analyze the whole thing in her head while she was sharing. I could tell this was bothering her but not enough to let him go.

"And they say women are complicated!" I said with a little laugh.

"I know right," Vi replied with a sigh. "I'm glad that we can talk about this stuff. Up to now I was on my own."

"Don't give up, Vi. If you care about him, keep at it," I advised. "You light up around him. He makes you laugh. Give it time." I carried on. "My friends Brian and Becca fought their attraction and their need to be with one another for so long that it was volcano when the emotions came out. They are now married with a beautiful baby on the way and they are happy. If you have happy in your life, Vi, don't let it go."

"Okay, but if a volcano erupts you're on my side!" she laughed and I had to laugh too.

We said our goodbyes and I walked over to Satan's Pride to meet my man. Guard said he had a surprise for me. I begged for a hint and he said to dress in jeans and boots. Not much of a hint but when he added "angel" and "your ass rocks those jeans," well, I didn't much care anymore.

So I rocked my jeans, black ankle boot and black tank top and black jacket. I pulled my hair back into a high ponytail, going for that sleek, clean feel. I sauntered into main common area to find the crew either playing pool gabbing, playing cards and whatever goes on behind the door off the main area. The few other times I have been there I saw some pretty questionable women coming out of there. It bothered me but the club has its world and Guard and I had ours.

I asked Demon, "Hey! Guard around here?"

# Guard

Demon is not much of a talker; as a matter of fact I don't think I ever heard him speak. He pointed to the office off to the side. He also rarely smiled but I think I got the best version I had seen from him as he pointed.

"Thanks." And I made my way to the office. I knocked because it was polite.

"Yeah." I heard my impatient man inside.

"It's me, honey. Do you want me to come back a little later?" I asked on the other side of the door.

The door was yanked open and an arm sneak out and pull me roughly. I was dragged up against a very hard body and sweet delicious lips.

"Hi, honey," I said softly against his mouth.

Guard continued to plunder my mouth with his deep, sensual tongue. Feels so good. I dropped my purse and moved my hand to grip the hair at the base of his neck; pulling keeping him close and moaning into his mouth.

Guard finally broke our kiss. His eyes were brilliant, his teeth hit my bottom lip once more and he felt my body shudder.

"Was this my surprise? 'Cause it if is, I do not understand the need for jeans." I teased.

He laughed out loud and I am sure the roar carried into the other room. "I love what those jeans do for me, baby, but it would not have been my first choice if I had dirty office sex in mind."

I blushed and he bent down to kiss my reddening cheek.

"I'm taking you for a ride," he said.

I grabbed my purse off the floor just in time to have him tag my hand and lead me out to the common room. We almost collided with a scantily clad woman. I thought she was extremely pretty. Blonde hair with too many highlights, but pretty none the less. I found angry blue eyes penetrating at Guard and me. Angry eyes has very petite figure and I knew this because she was showing most of it.

It took a few seconds but figured the angry eyes were directed to me. I figured this out because when she looked at Guard her face looked like a cat ready to purr.

"Hey, baby, it's been a long time, lover," Miss Bleached Blonde purred.

Now I am not a happy Ava.

Guard barked, "Not interested." He made a move to walk around her pulling me behind him.

Then she directed her attention to me and grabbed my other arm as I walked by, making me stop. "You think you could hold him for long, bitch? You would have better luck if you let me play with you two."

I know I was standing there with my mouth hanging open. Was she serious? Did she just say that like it was a common thing and that this were an everyday occurrence?

"Shut it!" I heard Guard say.

"Baby, she's too 'vanilla' for you. Do the poor little thing a favour and let her loose now. She doesn't have enough fight to be your old lady," purred the bleached bimbo.

"Darcy, I said shut it and get gone." Guard was getting angry.

I yanked my hand free of the both of them. No fight! Is she fucking kidding? She has no idea who or what I am. I am getting peeved again.

I stand between them as they continue to exchange words when I finally had enough of that.

"Darcy, is it? So let me get this straight. I have no fight, I am too vanilla and obviously can't hold Guard's attention. Did I get that right?" I asked, directing myself to stand right in front of her, pulling her attention from Guard.

"That's right, bitch," Darcy spewed.

"Right, so get this. I fight when necessary. I see no need to fight if Guard's made his choice. Also, vanilla or not, which is none of your fucking business, I refuse to belittle myself by showing up and talking like a prison inmate out on parole." I kept going. "If and I do mean if, Guard chooses to move on I would let him go. Not because I don't deserve him but because he deserves to be happy."

I took a breath and finished with, "Sometimes not fighting is the best thing you can do for someone. So I may not fight but I am stronger than you could ever imagine."

"Please, you think you have staying power?" came from Darcy.

"Life is fleeting, I'll take right here and right now." I looked over at Guard. "I'm ready for our ride now. You good to go?" I asked.

He pulled me close and put his arm around me. His hand fisted my hair and pulled my head back to kiss me soundly on the lips.

"What was that for?" I asked breathlessly.

"Being real, angel. I love that about you." And he kissed me again.

Our ride was beautiful. I had never been on the back of a Harley and it was amazing. I love the humming of the engine, the freedom of riding but my favourite part of all was having a reason to wrap my arms around Guard and press close to him. I let my hands roam over his chest until he grabbed them and told me to "be good." I thought I was being good. My hands could have headed in the other direction.

We reached our destination. He took me to a stream surrounded by wild-flowers. It was like a picture out of a painting. He helped me off the bike and took me to the edge of the stream. The rocks were braced against the edge of the water and Guard sat on one and pulled me to sit with him my back into his front, his legs splayed out and my head leaning back onto his shoulder.

"This is my place, angel. This is where I go when I want to be alone," he said in a quiet husky voice.

I took a deep breath and exhaled. I needed to tell him. I wanted him to know. I twisted to turn myself around and I was on my knees between his legs. My hands framing his face, and I looked directly into his eyes.

"Gabriel, stay quiet and just listen. No response is necessary; I just want you to know." I took another breath and said quietly against his lips, "I'm falling in love with you." I kissed him softly.

I started to separate my lips from his when his arms came around me like steel to hold me right where I was.

"Angel, you are in love with me." This was a statement, not a question. "I know this and you gotta know that I love you. Fuck, baby, I knew outside Satan's Pride when you took a stand with girly attitude."

OH, MY GOD! He loves me!

"Really?" I whispered. I wrapped my arms around his neck and pressed myself close.

"Yeah, baby, really." He kissed me and continued kissing me.

"Honey, this is not the most comfortable place to, um…you know," I said softly in his ear.

"Don't know, baby, uncomfortable for what?" He rose an eyebrow teasingly.

I plucked up my courage and found my inner diva and said, "I wanna fuck you. And to be more explicit, first I want to fuck you and then I want to fuck you dirty." I emphasized the "dirty."

It didn't take long for Guard to take me home and taught me another get lesson in fucking dirty.

# Chapter 11
# Baby Talk

Such a warm feeling snuggled tightly against Guard. Yet this annoying sound of continuous ringing blathers in my head. I reluctantly force my eyes open and automatically my eyes shift to my alarm. Three o'clock in the morning! I don't care who it was, I was going to kill them.

"Hello?" I managed to say in a rough hazy-not-quite-awake voice.

"Ava, it's time."

"What? Time for what? Who is this?" Clearly I am still unable to focus. Guard was stirring next to me. He has turned on the bedside lamp and was clearly waiting for me to tell him what crazy person calls at three in the morning.

"Ava, wake the fuck up! It's Brian! Becca is in labour and we're at the hospital. You promised to be here for her and I am not having my wife upset, so get your ass here," declared a very agitated Brian.

"Brian, I'm up. I will pack something and check the fastest route. Text me which hospital you're at and I'm there," I told him. "Keep Becca calm; tell her I'm on my way!" I assured him yawning and ended our call.

I saw Guard getting out of bed. "Angel, where's your overnight bag?"

"Um, closet," I replied rubbing my sleepy eyes.

"Pack, baby." He pulled out his cell phone and said, "I need a bag packed. Three days' worth. We'll swing by in half-hour to pick it up. I'll fill you in and leave instructions for the clan meeting." Guard clicked it off and looked at me still in bed staring up at him.

"Baby, we gotta move," he said and reached put to caress my cheek.

I jumped off the bed and thank goodness he was prepared to catch me. I wrapped my arms around his neck and legs around his waist. "You're coming with me. Thank you, honey." I stared into his eyes with my welding up with tears. He didn't hesitate or make excuses; he made time for me and my best friends and is making sure I get there safe. "I love you, Gabriel," I whispered in his ear, and then kissed him soundly on the mouth.

"Shit, angel, you keep that up and that baby is going to be four before we see it." He laughed.

I got dressed and packed in fifteen minutes, a record for me I might add. I accomplished this mainly because Guard was commandeering the situation and moving things along. We swung by Satan's Pride, picked up his bag and took to the road in my car. Guard drove and wanted to be useful so I tried to keep him amused. I told him about the kids in dance class and what comes out of their mouths. I let him know that I have found out more about mommies and daddies in this town that I really had no business knowing because kids pick up everything that's said. I also let him know that I was going to be very careful about how much I let my kids hear when daddy and I are spending time together.

Then, I told him about my mom and dad and my life growing up. I told him how my mom looked at dad like there was never anyone else in the room. Dad on the other hand doted on mom. He made sure that he always surprised her with trinkets. They didn't have to be expensive but little things that made her happy like her favourite scent of candles, running a bubble bath or just reading to her at night so she could cuddle into him and relax.

I am pretty sure I succeeded in amusing him with my story about my first school dance. I was fifteen and went with Ronald Hawthorne. He was utterly amused when I told him I had to explain to his parents how he got a broken nose.

"You broke his nose? Didn't know you had it in you." He was roaring with laughter.

"He grabbed my boob. Just to show off. I will not be objectified," I defended.

"I would have liked to see you slug him. Do I call you Rocky now?" he teased.

"Stop it or I make you go down for the count," I teased back.

It was two coffees and bagel stops later that we made it to the hospital. We made our way to the waiting room to find Becca's parents nervously sitting and looking at the main doors leading to the hospital rooms to catch sight of Brian.

# Guard

"Hello, Mr. and Mrs. Sullivan," I said.

Mrs. Sullivan jumped from her seat to hug me tightly.

"You're here, dear. Becca was asking about you."

Mrs. Sullivan suddenly stopped and looked beyond me looking over my shoulder and then up. She eyes were open wide and deflected her gaze from me to Guard. At the same time I noticed Mr. Sullivan standing right behind his wide with his hands on her shoulders.

I quickly looked at Guard and slipped my hand in his. I beamed proudly, "Mr. and Mrs. Sullivan, this is Guard."

Guard low dreamy voice uttered, "A pleasure to meet you both."

Mr. Sullivan reached over to shake Guard's hand and replied, "Call me Grant. This is Leslie." He indicated to his lovely wife.

"My, but you are a big man," was what came from Leslie Sullivan.

Thank goodness Guard chuckled.

Just then Brian came into the waiting room. "Ava, you're here, we're just about to go into the delivery room and Becca wanted me to see if you were here. You got two minutes before we go down. She wants to talk to you."

"How about I buy you both a cup of coffee?" Guard asked the Sullivans and directed them to the elevator. He slipped his hand around my neck and kissed softly. "We'll be back up in a few minutes and I will bring you a coffee. You want something else?"

"No, honey, coffee's good."

I followed Brian down the hall to see our Becca lying in bed very agitated.

"Sweetie, I'm here," I said to Becca.

She looked relieved to see me.

"Oh, thank goodness. I want you here. I need to tell you something." She looked so anxious. She was in her hospital gown and looking very uncomfortable but a small fake smile crossed her lips.

"Listen close! If it's a boy and I am too out of it to fight, you cannot let them call my baby Noel or Josie if it's a girl. We decided on names. If it's a boy it is Avery Holden Duncan and if it's a girl it's Ava Holly Duncan. Brian and I want to you to know how important you are in our lives and want to name our baby after you in some way. Don't let my parents have a say!" Becca commanded.

Tears streaming down my face, "I promise, sweetie. Anything you want, my darling girl." I held her hand until the orderly and nurses came to escort Becca to delivery with Brian by her side.

I made my way back into the waiting room, still wiping away my tears. I sat down and looked around. Hospitals have always frightened me. I was reliving the memories of coming to the hospital to see my parents to find out they had passed before I had the chance to say goodbye or tell them how much I loved them. I remember the nurses trying to console me, the look of pity in their eyes.

I did this once more when James was taken from me. I remember the pain of being alone again. Losing someone I loved again. More sadness and more loneliness. In fact, there was a time, after Becca asked me to be at the hospital that I was dreading my promise to come. I often thoughts of ways to get out of my vow to be there with them.

I was here, again, for a birth. A renewal of life and a reminder that in all things we can find a glimmer of light. As much as I have seen and felt such pain here, I am seeing the thrill of new parents and grandparents. I can see the love and tenderness that Brian is showing to his beautiful new mamma wife. So brilliant the way they look at each other.

An arm wraps around my shoulder. "Baby, you okay?"

I can see a concerned Guard looking down on me.

"Yeah, honey. I have some not so great memories here. Today I am trying to replace them with good ones." I tried to pass of a weak smile.

He held me tighter and kissed my forehead. "All memories serve a purpose. Some are to remind us of what we had and some to remind us of what we have learned. Others are to remind us to be grateful for all that we have become. Embrace them all, angel, make them your strength."

Several hours later, Avery Holden Duncan presented himself to our wonderful world. A beautiful baby with round cheeks and tiny bow lips and the sweetest baby smell.

I fell in love with Avery. I fell even more in love with Gabriel Guard Stone while he cautiously held little Avery in his arms. A giant man holding a tiny seven-pound four-ounce baby was an adorable sight to see. Seeing the look on my Gabriel's face was painfully beautiful. It reached my heart and I melted. It was even more perfect than when I held the baby. Although I must say there is a complete awesomeness to having a little person hold your finger so tightly.

We checked into a hotel for the night near the hospital to get some much need rest. Poor Guard, he did all the driving and was my rock today. Guard was already in bed when I snuck in beside him and turned out the bedside light.

"Thank you, honey, for everything today," I said as I caressed his chest with my fingertips. "I love you, Gabriel."

"I love you too, my beautiful Ava," he replied. "Avery looked good in your arms, baby. You are a natural."

"Think we should steal him and take him home with us?" I teased.

"Nah," he whispered softly, "Think we should make one of our own."

I went still. "You want a little Satan's Pride or two?"

"Yeah, you?"

"I do. I just never thought it was in the cards so I stopped thinking about it," I admitted. "I'm thirty-five, honey. I'm sure that I don't have that much time left," I whispered.

Guard lifted me and had me straddling him. He brought my face down to his so that we were eye to eye, nose to nose. "Maybe we get started then. I want to plant my baby in you. What do you say to that?"

The thought of carrying Guard's baby made my belly flutter! Oh, my, a precious baby with Gabriel would be my perfect world. It's almost too perfect to ask for, but I did anyway.

"I want that, Guard. I want a baby as beautiful and strong as you with precious eyes," I whispered.

"Or a little baby angel like my Ava. Sweet, smart and goofy."

"I'm not goofy," I said scrunching my nose.

"Long day today, baby. Let's start that baby in the morning," he snickered and pulled me down for a kiss then settled me into his chest as I stretched over him.

When we woke we got busy trying to make our baby.

# Chapter 12
# Big Boys Talking

B rian has done a spectacular job with the nursery. It was painted in pale yellow with green wide stripes. The room was filled with bright colourful toys. A huge teddy bear that little Avery won't be able to drag around until he is three and another adorable little bear from his Auntie Ava and Uncle Guard. The crib and change table were a deep mahogany, simple and elegant.

They released Becca and baby Avery the morning after. This completely shocks me as just a day ago Becca was in labour and to think how quickly our bodies can recover from giving birth to looking after precious helpless little baby. Becca placed Avery in his basinet and like any normal adults we stared in awe as this little man entertains us with little sigh of contentment. Absolute peace!

We tiptoe out of the room, well Becca and I tip toe, no way Guard or Brian would ever tip toe.

"Let me make you some lunch and I will prepare some simple meals so that you have back up dinners for the next couple of weeks," I told Becca. "Go have a lie down while you can and I'll call you when it's done."

I urged Becca to her bedroom. It didn't take a whole heck of a lot of convincing considering she was exhausted and sore.

"You two, out of the kitchen." I pointed to Brian and Guard. "I have to work fast if we are heading back tomorrow and I need a little quiet and some space. You are both on baby duty if he fusses."

I got down to it. I worked furiously in the kitchen for the next four hours. I made a whole pot of tomato sauce and divided it up into portions for smaller meals. I made a chili, beef stew and a few casseroles. This should see them through for a bit. I also made some baked chicken and salads for lunch and seeing as it's a little past one o'clock I timed that well.

I walked out to see where everyone was at and saw Brian cuddling little Avery in his arms on the leather couch in the den. Guard was sitting opposite them.

"This is the best. A beautiful wife, a perfect baby boy, I have it all," said Brian.

"You have it all," Guard confirmed, and then added, "I want that. I want this with Ava."

Oh, my God! He told me this but to admit this to Brian made this very real. Guard wants a family with me. My heart is pounding and tears are filling my eyes.

"Brian, you are the closet family to Ava, right?" he asked.

"Yeah, there are some distant cousins but she never really connected with them. Why?" Brian asked.

"I want to do it right," Guard said.

"Do what right?" Brian countered.

"I want to marry Ava and I want make sure I do it right," Guard said quietly.

"I don't make Ava's decisions, man. God knows I tried to sometimes but Ava is Ava. She's gonna follow her heart. I will tell you this, she loves you. I see it. Bec sees it. It's real. And saying that, I will also tell you that she has been through more loss and pain than anyone should have to endure. So if you are serious then I am good but if you fuck with her, even with your band of merry men, I will find you and I will beat the shit out of you. She may not be my blood sister but she is my sister." Brian's tone was sincere and serious.

"If I fuck this up, I want you to find me and put me out. I have told her all my shit. All of it! She never even blinked. Put her arms around me and told me she with me. She knows the club has rules and she hates the term old lady but she deals with it. She fights me on what's really important to her that's when I know I need to pull back." Guard stands up and runs a hand through his hair. "I don't want her away from me, not for one day. I left the club to deal with shit for a high profile meeting so that I could be here. Two months ago, not a fucking chance I would have left, especially not for a woman."

My heart was fluttering and I was backing out of the room. He loves me and he wants a family with me. Those were not just words last night in the heat of the moment. He loves me. And I adore him.

I take a breath to hustle back in making plenty of noise this time. "Guys, lunch is ready!" I bellowed from the hallway. I met them at the doorway to the kitchen. "Give me my little man, I will put him down and call Becca for lunch." I hopped upstairs, my heart light and filled with sunshine.

# Chapter 13
# Ring of Fire

Guard and I made it home with lots of pictures and memories of baby Avery's first few days. I got promises from both Brian and Becca that I would receive pictures weekly of our sweet boy. As always I found it hard to leave great friends and the only family I truly had, but this time was easier than others because I was coming home with Guard.

I was looking forward to Milly's coffee and my heart to heart's with Vi. I loved my little grocery store and the personal assistance from Eddie and the gang.

I found myself thinking about my Satan's Pride boys and how I started the weekly BBQ ritual that they loved. They would bring the meat and do a BBQ but I would add the biscuits, salads, pasta and always make slew of desserts. I was getting texts from Orion or War asking if we were having one that weekend. I confirmed and warned them since I was gone it there may not be as many options. I got a smiley face in return. I had to giggle, big biker bad asses sending smiley faces.

Guard was calmer and we have settled into a beautiful groove. He would spend most nights at home with me and on occasion when he needed to be at the club, we would still make the time to see each other that day. He is the first thing I wanted to see in the morning and the last I wanted to be with at night. I was even sleeping better.

Our BBQ was well underway and I always extended the invitation to girlfriends and wives. I found out that there weren't that many of us. So we became a tight little group of five women that drank margaritas as the crew barbecued. Dianne was married to Zer (the most serious crew member and the tech guy of the crew). Gemma was Jarr's woman. Jarr was the scout of the crew and kept up with what was happening with the surrounding clubs. Mara had just met Crick and was having a tough time adjusting to the whole Satan's Pride brotherhood. They met when Crick was beaten by a rival crew six months back and she was his nurse. And of course there is Vi and myself.

I was sitting at the fire pit watching the flames lick upwards. I liked to watch the dancing flames. I felt Guard at my back. He wrapped himself around me. His arms and legs encasing me to him. I lean back to have my head rest to one side on his shoulder.

"Whatcha thinking, angel?" he murmured in my ear as he kisses me right there.

"It's a beautiful dancing story, honey," I replied in a small voice.

"What?"

"The fire, honey, it dances. It's like me. It depends on the elements that surround it but it adapts and dances swaying in that moment. It's telling us a story. Each dance is unique and magnificent," I explained.

"Yeah, baby. It dances just like you. Magnificent, just like you," he whispered in my ear.

It was a wonderful night ending with the sweetest lovemaking. So tender that I lay in bed with gentle tears sliding down my cheeks. I fell asleep enveloped in strong arms and a sensuous tongue licking at my neck and shoulders. I revelled in the magical sensation of our two bodies together.

Not long before, Guard undressed me slowly, manipulating my body with kisses. Slow, tormenting kisses all over my breasts, hips, and legs, leaving no place untouched or un-kissed. My body was aching for him. I whispered and begged for him to come inside.

"Not done tasting you, angel. On your belly, baby." He rolled me onto my belly and the onslaught continued. I was coming undone. I thought I was going to die from the excruciating sensual torture.

Guard guided his lips and tongue across the back of my neck, sweeping my long dark hair out of his was to the side but lightly fisting his hand in it to keep me still. Those lips moved across my shoulders and down my spine, stopping at the base. He felt his lips and tongue sweep against each ass cheek as his hands ran down the sides of waist. His hands moves down the crevice of my ass and slowly parted my legs as the assault continued.

I still go warm just thinking of how Guard ran his lips and tongue to the inside of my thighs. I felt a pillow slide under my belly and he slid my legs further and further apart. His fingers found my wet pussy and slid in, working them in a circle until he heard my breath hitch and a deep moan emitted from me. My head fell forward and my hips lifted to get more of his fingers. He slid two fingers inside and a slow easing pressure of in and out while his lips moved closer and closer to join his fingers.

"Honey, I need more," I said huskily.

"Yeah? What do you need, angel?" I feel his breath against my sex.

"You. Please, honey. More." I panted out those words. I was reaching and reaching for that ultimate release.

"You want me baby, I'm here." And with those words he positions my body elevating it so that he is blanketing me with his body and I feel him slide inside. Ever so slowly. Excruciatingly slow and steady.

"Faster," I whispered.

"Hush, baby. I want it slow," he growled in my ear.

I hushed and gripped the sheets tighter with each slow powerful thrust.

I felt his hands lace into mine and kiss my neck again before his hips thrust hard inside me. Hard long thrusts mover faster and faster. I moaned and tensed. I was closed.

"Let me have that moan, baby. I wanna hear it all," he urged.

I let loose. Holding on tightly to his hands laced in mine and I hear Guard's primal grunt and release. Our bodies still connected.

The most beautiful moment I had ever felt.

*Two Weeks Later*

I was getting more and more eager to ride on Guard's bike with him. I was becoming a motorcycle junkie. Actually, my favourite part is wrapping my arms around him. Our first stop whenever we ride together is the rocks. We sit on the rocks and sometimes we talk and sometimes we just sit and look at the water. Today I could see that he had something on his mind.

"Do you remember our first conversation, angel?"

I was busy tasting his divine jaw with little kisses that I only replied, "Mmm hmm." I allowed myself to nuzzle into his neck.

"What did I say, baby?"

"You said I belong to you, all of me. Why are you asking, honey?"

"Are you mine, angel?" Guard's piercing blue eyes looking deeply into mine, arms wrapped tightly around me as I straddled him on our special rock.

"I only want to be with you. I want to be yours if you want me to be. And I want you to be mine," I said with a little swallow.

"You'll wear my patch? You'll be my old lady?" he asked with a sly grin, knowing that I still disliked the term "old lady."

Staring into those pools of blue I took a breath. "I would wear your patch proudly, honey. I will also let you call me 'old,'" I said with a scrunch to my nose. "I would do anything for you."

"Anything?" he said suspiciously. "Will you dance with me?"

"Here?"

He stands on the rock and takes me with him. His arms around me and we take a few steps together on the rock as Guard hums in my ear. I look up at him and smile. He's so sweet.

"I love you," I said softly as I reach up to touch the hair at the base of his neck.

"Hands in mine, baby," he commanded.

I complied. I feel his fingers slide something through mine.

I look down to see a breathtaking brilliant ring. A beautiful oversized princess cut ruby surrounded by diamond with diamonds all along the band in platinum. It is exquisite.

My mouth trembled and I raised my eyes to his beautiful badass biker face. Tears in my eyes, I wrapped my arms around him and tip toed and pulled him down at the same time so our lips meet.

"Mine," he said.

"Mine," I returned.

OMG! I am engaged to the most wonderful, sexiest man.

# Chapter 14

# Wire's Obsession

The Satan's Pride crew had heard our news and Vi came visiting a few days later. The badass dudes of Satan's Pride seem to be happy for Guard and me. This makes me happy because they are Guards brothers and respect and loyalty are the crux of their club. I take this very seriously because Guard is the president and I need to be a strong support to him and his crew.

We called Brian and Becca to tell them the good news and they were thrilled for us. They also wanted share some news and asked us to be godparents to Avery. We agreed without hesitation.

It seems like my life has gone from grey to a beautiful rainbow of colours.

Final class for the evening was complete and they kids have all been picked up by parents. I closed off the studio and headed back to the house to make a late dinner for Guard and myself. I thought I would make a simple dish of chicken and rice so that I could get some paperwork done at the same time.

I was completely engrossed in my task of balancing the books when I heard the doorbell ring. I wasn't expecting anyone except my handsome fiancée and he has a key. I went to the door and followed Guard's instructions to a tee. Check the peephole, nothing there. Make sure the light is on and check through the windows, still nothing to be seen. I was beginning to think I was hearing things.

I pulled myself back into the kitchen, and called Guard.

"Honey, are you almost here?" I asked with a slight degree of tension.

"Yeah, angel, just about there," he replied. Thank God for Bluetooth. "Everything all right?"

"Yes, just want you home." I tried to keep the edginess out of my voice.

"Coming up the drive now, baby."

"Okay, I'll meet you at the door."

I scrambled off the phone and ran to the front door to see the lights of his ride turn off. I whipped open the door to find an envelope stuck to it. I pulled it off and read the note on the cover. "Ava, read when alone. Urgent! Confidential."

I hint of panic crossed over me and I decided that I would read it later tonight and then share with Guard later.

I hid the note between the pages of the book, sitting on the coffee table I was reading and got back to the door in time to kiss my man. I led him into the kitchen and set the table for our serene intimate dinner. We found ourselves in the living room later sunk into the sofa, I was half lying on Guard watching a movie and relaxing as our hands fit snuggly around one another.

The next day after Guard and I had breakfast together on the patio and he left for the shop, I had the opportunity to re-visit the envelope still tucked away safely in the book.

"If you want Guard and Satan's Pride to cease to exist ignore this. I want to see you alone behind the gas station just outside of Stewart and Dons Road at 2 P.M. today. You have a choice to make." It was signed Wire.

Oh my God, oh my God. I sat in shock.

What do I do? I clutch the letter to my chest trying to breathe air into my lungs.

Guard is my love and my happiness. Satan's Pride is my family. Those brothers have looked after me, supported me and accepted me.

Do I tell Guard? It would be a war. This could mean bloodshed and it would be my fault. I can't think!

I looked at the note over and over again. I have spent all day agonizing over whether to tell Guard or not. Okay, maybe I am overreacting. I take this meeting and then tell Guard at least I will know what he's after.

It was 1:20 and I have to leave in a few minutes if I am going to meet Wire. I feel like throwing up. My heart is racing. How do I protect myself? How do they find me if something happens?

I quickly texted Vi. "Meet you at the diner at 3 P.M. Hugs, Ava."

# Guard

I got in my SUV and head out to the meeting place. I was glad it was broad daylight and I knew there was traffic on this street and it was a busy gas station.

I got there at 2:05 P.M. to find Wire and another biker by their Harley's. Wire sat there staring at me drive in. He never took his eyes off me. I made sure to park facing them and stepped out of my vehicle.

"Hey, pretty dancer." Wire's voice made my skin crawl. I wanted to jump back into my car and take off.

I said nothing and stayed by my car.

"Come closer. I don't bite." It was a command.

"You can tell me what you want from right there," I said and pointed to where he was standing, hopefully in a more confident voice than I heard in my own head.

"Scared?" he taunted.

"Smart," I replied.

"Never let it be said that I don't compromise. You take two steps forward and I will take one step forward. Close enough for me to talk and you to feel safe." He's negotiating.

The thought of getting closer to him made my skin crawl but I also didn't want to show him any fear.

I thought a moment. "Okay." I waited for him to move forward and then I did.

"What do you want?" I asked, my eyes meeting cold ones.

"In a hurry?" he asked

"Yes, actually, I have to meet someone."

"Guard?" He twisted the name out of his mouth with venom.

"None of your business but no," I said calmly. "I will only ask this once more, what do you want?"

"I want you," he threw out roughly.

Fuck!

I started to walk backward when I heard, "I would listen up before your fiancé and brothers aren't breathing."

I stopped but held my ground and waited for him to say something.

"Guard won't play to my request in partnering and transporting some delicate cargo through Satan's Pride territory. It's pissing me off. Now I have a few options. I can call the rival clubs and start a major problem. Or I can find another way to settle the score."

"And you think I would sleep with you? Not a chance," I stated firmly.

"It was my first choice. Didn't think you'd go for it," he sneered.

"You're right, so what do you want?" I said.

"I want my own private performance. You dance for me, where I choose and in what I choose." He smirked.

"Why would I do that?" I asked

"Because looks like you may want to keep him in one piece. You do, I move on, you don't I will take each member down one by one." The sick twisted bastard meant every work. I could see it in his face. "You have twenty-four hours. You'll find another note with a time and place. You don't show I find another way to entertain myself. Crapshoot who I target first." He was cruel and each word came out like toxin.

I didn't even respond. I got in my car and left. I parked just outside of town and let the dam of tears burst through.

What choice do I have? If I tell Guard there will be bloodshed. What if he finds out? He will never understand.

He'll walk away from us.

But he'll be alive. He will be safe. I can't let anything happen to him.

I love him. I feel more for him than I have ever felt for anyone. More than James and I loved James very much. But nothing compares to what I feel for Gabriel "Guard" Stone.

I look at my ring and stare at the precious red stone. The beautiful symbol from Guard to signify the fire we shared for one another and our personal dance together.

Guard taught me to love again and to love fully.

I need to compose myself, meet Vi and make my night with Guard the beautiful we have ever had. After tonight I may not have him anymore.

I meet with Vi. I work hard to make sure that I keep up the pretence so that no one was wise about my impending doom.

I am sure that Vi knew that I was not myself. I smiled and drank coffee and chatted about all the talk and gabby things girls chat about. Vi was keen and never asked if there was something wrong but searching my face for clues.

I stayed quiet about what was really bothering me.

# Chapter 15
## A Night to Remember

I waited at in the bedroom for Guard. I lay a trail for Guard to entice into my bedroom. I wanted tonight to be exceptional. No matter what happens tomorrow I want tonight to be about us.

I kept the lights dim in the living room. A trail of undergarments on the railing and stairs leading up to our bedroom and for a hint of mystery I left a red silk scarf tied on the doorknob.

Candles were lit all over the room. I decided to wait on the bed in red lace panties and matching bra. I left my hair in loose curls and left my makeup light but made sure to accentuate my lips with a read shade of lipstick.

Guard always tells me how he loved my high heels. So I finished off my barely there outfit with a pair of silver open toed heels. I want tonight to be a memory I can cling to if and goes awry and my beautiful happy world falls apart.

I am positive that Wire will not make it as simple as a private dance just for him. My mind has evolved and has formulated the opinion that he will find a way to make this known to Guard. Will he believe me? Will he forgive me?

I have made a plan of my own when I meet Wire but tonight I do not want think of him.

Tonight is for me and Guard.

I have been listening for the front door to open and I finally hear the key in the lock. Guard usually makes his way to the kitchen first. True to form I can hear his footsteps heading that way. By this point he has found my note. I kept it simple.

"Come find me, honey. Tonight is all about you," it read.

I can hear him at the bottom of the stairs where I left my jeans, and I can hear the footsteps coming up the stairs, pausing ever few steps and he finds my shirt, bra and panties. I know he is standing on the other side of the door.

I see the doorknob turn and lay on my side in our bed. He standing in the doorway and takes a step in. He drops all the clothes he's found leading up the stairs and glances around the room at the flickers of soft light illuminated by the candles.

His gaze finds its way to me. I stay perfectly still. His eyes are filled with a bright fire, his jaw tight and as I glance down to his bulge I could see how restricted it must be.

The silence is too much. I wanted him to come to me.

I stretch out my hand. "Honey, come to me," I said with a slightly shaky voice, my eyes meeting his.

"Angel, let me enjoy this. Don't move, baby," he said with a smooth husky voice. He continued to stare and as he did this he removed his t-shirt. My eyes followed every curve of every muscle on his body. His boots thud to the floor and he moves towards me waiting for him.

A knee hits the bed and I notice the red scarf in his hands. "On your back, baby," Guard commanded. I can feel the wetness between my legs with just the sound of his voice.

I complied, my breathing already becoming laboured. I felt the soft silk scarf drift across my body, teasing and tantalizing my senses. He asked in a whispered voice, "All about me?"

"Anything you want." My body was aching for him to touch me. My be-traying body moved under the touch of the silky scarf.

"Anything?" he continued, as he pulled my lower lip between his teeth.

I was coming undone. Guard has barely touched me and I am quivering from head to toe.

"Mm, anything, honey." I murmured in a low moan.

"Stay still." Then Guard proceeded to tie the scarf around me eyes as a blindfold. He maneuvered my hands over by head, palms upwards. He hands were igniting me as he slid them down my arms, down my side, moving past my thighs, slithering down to my ankles. With a sudden jolt, Guard spreads my legs wide, making me gasp. I can feel my breasts heaving and my body tingling with anticipation of his move.

"Still. Do. Not. Move." Each word was emphasized in a deep low growl by my ear.

Then I hear him at the door and quick paces down the stairs. Surely he wasn't going to leave me now. I notice the sounds of clinking and cupboards. The steps coming upward seem heavily. The door opens and I hear, "My beautiful angel is being good."

What has he brought with him? There is shuffling and then I sense the bed dip once again. I can feel Guards thighs on either side of my hips pressing in. I lick my lips in anticipation of his next move. I feel the tip of his nose against mine, then feel it slide to my cheek and over to my ear. His breath teasing my face with every movement.

"Is this pretty lace bra for me?" he asks against my ear.

"Yes," I gasped.

"To do as I want?" he presses.

"Yes."

"Pretty red lace, very delicate against your skin. Looks beautiful." Then he encloses a nipple in his mouth and tugs over the lace bra.

I moan and move my head to the side. Immediately Guard takes his mouth away from me.

"Still," he growled. I move my head back, partly because his growl was intense and partly because I needed his mouth back on me.

I was quickly rewarded with the return of his mouth, first tugging and nipping. This was followed by teasing licks and then a sucking motion that became more and more driven. I thought I was about to burst and Guard moves his mouth to my other breast to give it the same attention and tenderness. This continued for what seemed an eternity. His mouth suddenly moves and I feel his hands on my breasts and he kneads them gently, then with one sudden action I feel him rip my bra down the middle and free me.

I gasp in shock. I hear his voice at my ear, "Still." And a little lick hits my ear. My body shudders.

I bite down on my lower lip to get control my body and remain still. His mouth finds my hard nipples again and the suckling recommences, pulling out moans from deep inside me. I don't move for my man. I stay still, just as my man requests. "My good girl."

Oh, God, those words alone almost made me come. A spasm hits me.

His mouth and tongue slide down over my stomach and abs. My body flinches ever so slightly but I was being so good, just as Guard wants. I feel his mouth moving lower to the apex of pussy. With legs sprawled wide and his tongue sliding over me pussy, I can't contain stop myself from begging for more.

"Honey, please."

"Hush, angel, I am savouring my beautiful pussy," he said while continuing to lick me thoroughly. Then in a sudden instant his mouth closes over my clit and the pressure of the lace and tongue made my hips jerk.

Guard stopped instantly. "Baby, you moved." He scolded lightly. His lips were at my ear. "How shall I punish you, baby?"

"Um…I don't know," I whispered, my body racking with need for his lips to find my again.

His hands roam my body and slide down to the sides of my panties. Again, with an unexpected yank, I am shocked to have my panties ripped from me. I cried out in surprise and his mouth silences mine. A long, wet, deep kiss.

Upon ending our kiss, I can feel Guard shift on the bed. "Angel, I want to make you scream for me."

With those words I feel a cold wet rock that I quickly clarify as ice being across my neck. Cold and yet it is burning me up. Over my breast travelled the ice and circling my hard nipples that have been teased mercilessly and are aching to be touched.

"Oh, please," I moaned in a slow drawl. The ice moves over my belly and settled in my navel, then over to one hip and then the other. It moved lower and lower until it nicked my clit. I would have jerked if Guard was not holding me down and steady. The ice continued to melt and circle my nub. I was so wet with need and I licked my lips and continue with straggled whimpers and pleas for release.

"Baby, you said this is all about me. I am not done yet discovering every sweet crevice. My sweet angel didn't know what she offered when she said "anything". I am taking everything, baby. I can see my pussy is dripping. Time for a taste."

His mouth closes over my pussy. Sucking deeply and intensely that I couldn't contain my thighs tensing and if it wasn't for Guard lying between then open them wide open and they would have left the bed. Instead I am pinned to the bed with this aggressive mouth making me expel harsh pants and pleas.

"Not yet. You can't come yet. I want my cock in your mouth." He growled as his mouth plundered and entered inside me. Darting in and out of my pussy, tongue fucking me.

A pained groan left my body and Guard let up and let his fingers move in and out of my pussy. I felt something at my mouth. "Lick it, baby." This is the first time Guard has wanted me to put his cock in my mouth. He would always let me stroke but always stopped me when I wanted it in my mouth.

I gladly lick my baby's smooth hard cock. I went to place the tip in my mouth and two fingers pushed hard inside my pussy. "Only licking for now," he said roughly. I wanted my man happy so I licked and licked until he allowed me to take his cock in my mouth and I sucked softly and allowed him to fill my mouth with him.

His fingers were assaulting me down below and I couldn't hang on any longer. Guard could sense this and felt my body shudder and my legs tense. My breathing was rapid. At the same time I could hear the effect I was having on Guard and the rough and ragged breath emitting from his lungs. He pulls his cock out of my mouth and his fingers away from my pussy.

I moan in disappointment at feeling left bereft of his contact. I feel his hand undo the silk and remove it from my eyes. "I want your eyes on me and your lips on mine as I make love to you, angel." He positions my legs over the back of his muscular thighs, placed his cock at my entrance and thrusts hard into me. I gasp harshly at the hardness and fullness I have inside me. It feels so good. Guard laces his hands in mine and as I catch my breath and with his eyes looking deeply into mine, he pulls out and then another hard thrust into the core of me. I am going to come apart.

"You ready for more of me? Hard and fast?" he asks. I can tell he has reigned himself in to let me adapt to his purposeful thudding inside.

"Yes, honey, give me everything, please," I begged. With that said, he was pounding inside me hard and fast and I came with thirty seconds of his first thrust, moaning harshly and finding that glorious place of ecstasy, my face in his throat and my teeth on his shoulder where I did not notice I had my teeth.

It was right after that when I heard Guard's body grunt and groans of primitive release. His hips bucking over me and into me and slowly having them slow down where his thrust becomes gliding between my legs. Guard pulls me into his arms and places me tucked at his side my arm over his chest and resting on his heart. I kiss his chest and let me hand roam over his abs and up to his chest.

Guard kisses the top of my head letting our breathing slow down to normal.

Lifting me over to straddle his legs and bringing my chest down to his so that our eyes meet, I hear his soft sexy voice, "Love that you did this. My sexy angel made me go wild tonight."

"I'm glad I make you happy, honey," and I kissed his nose then rubbed mine against his mimicking his actions.

"Not done being happy," he said gruffly and kissing me soundly on my mouth. "I got whatever I want all night. We are definitely not done yet." His hands round up around my ass and squeezes tightly and pulls me into him and grinds his hardening cock into me creating a tingling through my body.

"Go clean up, I wanna eat you again," he growled.

I looked in his eyes and saw the glint and my pussy automatically responded with a spasm that I am sure Guard felt. He loosened his grip and let me go into the bathroom to get cleaned up.

I made my way back to the bed and was pulled onto Guard and placed so that I was holding onto the headboard and my pussy was open for his mouth to taste. And he did this methodically taking all the time he needed. I brought me to the brink several times and pulled back until I cried out in frustration. Then he held me down hard and sucked and nipped until I hit my orgasm that lasted an immensely long time. He never stopped and when I was climbing down off my first orgasm he licked and sucked and held me down hard against his mouth and made me cry out again and five minutes later I came again. I wasn't able to hold onto the headboard any longer and I was leaning down over Guard. He slid me down over his body until my mouth hit his and I could taste myself on his lips.

I feel so naughty and get so damn good.

"I love those moans when you come, angel. Let's me hear that again."

Guard proceeded to build that passion again taking me over the edge of reason where he was the master of my body and I loved every moment of his mastery.

It was early morning and countless orgasms later that I lay exhausted in Gabriel's arms being stroked and caressed into a deep sleep.

# Chapter 16
## Best Laid Plans

**"**Angel, not that I don't appreciate the wild girl you showed me last night but is there a reason you gave me that?" Guard asked over our morning coffee. It was a ritual we started where we would sit on the patio on the lounge chair with Guard wrapped around me.

"You give me everything, honey. I wanted to give you more of me, something I would never and could never share with anyone else." I spoke softly. These words would never be truer and I hope he understand this when this day is done.

"You got something weighing you down?" he asked with his eyes searching my face.

I stroked his cheek and jaw and with my bravest voice, "No, Gabriel. I love you now and always."

"I love you too, angel," he responded still looking me over but said no more.

After my man left, I waited for Wire's instructions, secretly hoping that this would never come. I was not so lucky. A delivery man showed up with a package. I proceeded to open it and found gaudy, slutty tight hot pink tube top and short shorts that match. It was accompanied with a map to a location.

He must think I'm stupid. I turned on my computer and "Googled" the address to find this was one of his strip clubs just into the next town. I read Wire's note: "Looking forward to my private performance. Be here by 9 P.M. and alone."

I feel sick already and my stomach begins to heave. I have made some wonderful friends here in town and thought it was time to trust someone just in case all goes bad.

I got together all I needed. Placed it all in an oversized bag and headed into town. It was hours later when I made it home and I was satisfied that I had done all I could to minimize the fallout that may happen with the choice I was about to make.

I sat and contemplated not going. I picked up the phone to tell Guard all afternoon. Then I remember his words: "Crapshoot who I target first."

Fuck!

Guard has taken care of me and now I need to make sure he is safe.

I'm ready. I can do this. This is for my man and all he holds close.

The drive out of town is quiet. The sun is setting quicker now that we are hitting autumn. I love the colours on the trees and normally I would take the time to admire the wonders of nature but today my mind is filled with anxiety.

I park in the lot at the strip club and it's empty except for two bikes. The sign flashing says "Near Bare." How appropriate for a strip club, actually kind of witty so I was sure that Wire didn't think of it.

I think of Wire's intimidating face and stance and know that there is no light-heartedness and wit. I do know that he holds a grudge and wants his pound in flesh. There needs to be more of a history to these two clubs but every time I bring up the subject it becomes "club business" and I don't belong in it. Guard wants to keep the tainted past in the past.

It's 8:57; I need to get out of my car. I take one last look in the car mirror and remind myself that I am strong. I have been through deaths, sadness, loneliness and hurt. Guard pulled me out and made my life sweet and showed me passion. I will protect him because he has proven over and over that he takes care of me.

The dimly lit entrance led to a seedy room with worn out chairs resting on the tables. The floors felt sticky and I could see the stage was draped in cheesy blue velvet adorned by poles for the strippers to hang from. All but one table was empty, that is where I see Wire sitting with his feet resting on another chair. He was with one of his crew members identified by the marking emblems of flames and skull on their jackets. He was wearing black leather pants and red t-shirt and the typical black heavy motorcycle boots. I wore the jacket with the patch Guard gave me. It is my act of defiance, letting them know that I belong to Satan's Pride and to Guard.

# Guard

Upon hearing the click of my heels, they both turn their heads towards me. The salacious look in their eyes almost made me want to vomit right there. I managed to keep a cold facade and approached noting not to get too close. Wire was stroking his jaw and looking me over like he did that first night when I had the displeasure of making his acquaintance.

"I'm here," I said matter-of-factly.

"You are," he replied and looked me up and down. His demeaning pink outfit was on under my knee length jacket.

"So it's nine o'clock and I am here. I want to get this over with. I presume you want me on the stage and I assume we can get this underway." I was impersonal and my tone was stoic.

"Relax, little dancer, join me for a drink first." Wire's lips curved upwards into a smile. "What would you like?"

"I would like to get this over with. I would like for you to find a heart. I would like to go home to my man. I am assuming that none of this matters to you, so I prefer to get on with this. I am here for one dance in the costume of your choosing. Can we move on?" I kept reminding myself composure and tact.

"Listen, pretty girl, I am doing you a favour. I could have attacked by now and I want to savour this moment. The moment I know that what is Guard's was also mine." The words slithered out of his mouth like acid.

"I. Will. Never. Be. Yours." I said, punctuating each word, and then continuing, "You may have a brief fleeting moment of what you consider to be me but all you have is an act that I have supplied in many productions throughout. So tell yourself what you like but I belong to Guard." I begin walked past him to the stage steps.

"What makes you think you get to leave after this?" he says as he grabs my upper arm as I am walking past. His lethal eyes meet mine.

"Let go. This was not the deal." I was internally panicking but kept my voice steady.

"I hold the cards, maybe I change the deal." His hand tries to pull me closer and I resist.

"Not happening."

"You think you have a choice, pretty girl?" he laughs out loud right at me.

"Let go. Or this becomes an unpleasant experience for the both of us," I say calmly.

"You do as you're told or your band of nitwits pays the consequences. Simple as that." Now he pulls me closer and has both my arms in his steel like grip. "I think I want a kiss before the performance."

I struggle to pull away only to be hauled inches away from his face. I make the only move I remember from a self-defense class that Becca and I took years ago, and with the four-inch heel of my spiked shoe grind it into Wire's boot as hard as I can. I get enough of a reaction that he let's go and I turn to run.

I can hear him swearing and almost make it to the door when an arm reaches out and pulls me back and throws me in a chair. I try to gather my brainpower and before I can do anything I feel powerful thrust of a hand across my face, knocking my head back. I can feel the immense pain shoot up my cheek to my eye. I can taste blood. As I begin to open my eyes I feel another power hit on the other side of my face, once again knocking me backward.

I keep my eyes closed in an effort to keep out the pain. My arms are pulls back behind me and I can feel something binding them together.

"Not so pretty now, baby." I hear his voice in my ear. Bile forming in my throat, my face was aching and I couldn't move my arms. Panic was turning to fear.

"Maybe I send you back to Guard with a few more scars."

I continue to hear this vile sneer in my ear. I feel a smooth cold blade being traced along my cheek, and down my neck.

I feel it press in at my throat. The trickle of blood drips with the slight nick made from the blade. Wire was making his point. I pull in a breath and try as I might I cannot stop the tears formulating in my eyes and falling down my cheeks.

It was then that I felt his hand move down heading toward my breast; I try to wrestle myself away.

Wire grabs my face roughly with his hand. "You will take what I give." His eyes dark and filled with evil, his hand digging into my face.

A massive thud and crash turns Wire's head and I use my legs to push him away throwing my chair backward hitting the floor and knocking me to the floor with a violent jerk. I hear yelling, and fighting but my head is getting fuzzy and cloudy. I can barely focus when I hear Guard's voice. "Angel, stay with my angel."

# Guard

"Gabriel," I whisper. I feel my arms unlock from the binds. I am having trouble breathing. I can't keep my eyes open. I can hear the grunting and yelling along with fighting and it continues to getting fainter in my head.

"Baby, I'm here." His eyes searching mine but my eyes are drifting shut.

"I'm sorry, honey. Wanted to make it safe for you. I love you." My voice faded and then I felt black surround me.

# Chapter 17
## Recovering in Satan's Pride

My eyes feel heavy. I try to open them. My lids flutter a couple of times. I try again to open them completely and I am frustrated that I cannot keep them open. I sigh and resign myself that maybe I just need to keep them closed a little longer.

I feel warmth on my hand and a voice. Low and soft in tone, it's Guard. I can't make out the words but I can feel his stroking my hand. I want to let him know that I am here so I focus on my hand and lift my fingers and give a small whimper, "Guard."

I feel his lips on my hand and drift again into unconsciousness.

My head hurts. I feel like someone took a hammer to it. I can hear voices in the room. Who's here? I lift my hand to my forehead to try and get the thudding to stop. I work my eyes open and see the bright light and soft croaking moan leaves me.

Immediately the voices stop and they turn to me. I see Guard's face. Pale, tired eyes, scruffy stubble on his face. My poor man. He looks so worried. I lift my hand to his cheek and with tears falling from my eyes rolling down my cheeks, I whisper, "I'm sorry."

"Shh, angel. I'm here. My precious angel." Guard lowers his forehead to mine and takes in a deep breath. His lips kiss my forehead, nose and drift over my lips cautiously. He turns his head towards the door and says. "Let the nurse know she's awake."

Who was he talking to?

He turns back to me and says softly, "Baby, Becca, Brian and Avery are here." He looks over his shoulder and my eyes follow him. I see Becca standing with Avery in her arms with lips trembling ready to burst out in tears. She comes to the other side of me and takes my hand. "We were so worried, honey. When Guard called Brian couldn't drive here fast enough."

I look up at her and Avery. "I'm okay. No crying, Becca, you'll scare Avery." I try and tease but no being very successful.

"Turtle, you scared the life out of us!" Brian exclaims in a not-too-calm voice. "What the hell were you thinking?" He pulls his hand through his hair and continues. "There are people here who love you. Don't you dare ever pull a stunt like that ever again." Then just a loving brother does he moves around and kisses me on the cheek.

"I promise," I whisper. My eyes go back to Guard and I can see the tortured look in his eyes. I stroke his face. "Honey, I just wanted to protect you and the boys."

Guard draws in a deep breath. "We will talk about it later, baby. You need to rest now."

Brian, Becca give me quick kisses and head to the door. "We will be back later. After Avery is up from his nap we will come back to visit Auntie Ava."

As the Duncan clan walk out the door I see the nurse arrive with Vi and Orion following behind.

"Hello there, Ava, so glad to see those pretty eyes of yours." The nurse was sweet and gentle. Dressed in pink scrubs, and so attentive. You could tell that this was her passion and that each person she cared for was a priority. She was about my age and she looked around the room and smiled and greeted them all with a smiling, "Hello." Then proceeded with, "I need to check out our patient. Could I ask you all to give us a little privacy?"

Orion and Vi made their way to the door, Vi blows me a kiss and she tells me she'll be right back. Guard doesn't move. "NO.", he said emphatically. "Not leaving her alone anymore." He was still holding my hand and the determined on his face brought me to tears.

"Please let him stay," I said.

Nurse Ella, she introduced herself, said she would work around Guard and continued to do just that starting with checking all my vitals. Then she let me know where the injuries began.

"You have dislocated your collarbone, a severe concussion, sprained ankle and two cracked ribs. The good news is that all will heal just fine and you'll be back to your old self in six to eight weeks. In the meantime, you cannot go home without care though because we don't want you to be placed under any-more strain for the next couple of weeks. The doctor will be in to see you in the next hour or two and can let you know when you can be released." Nurse Ella patted my arm and let me know she would be back.

I gave her a weak smile and watched her walk out room. I turned back to Guard. His head was on the side of my bed and he was still holding my hand.

"Honey, you need to sleep." I move my other hand to stroke his hair.

"Not leaving."

"Then climb in bed with me and lay beside me."

"Don't want to hurt you." Guard voice was hoarse and tired.

"Please, honey; it's killing me to see you like this. Come lie with me," I coaxed.

I shifted my body over and tugged lightly on his arm. He gets up ever so slowly and gently pulls the wires and cords attached to aside and slides beside me.

"Close your eyes, honey."

I no sooner said the words when I felt and heard the steady pace of his breath. I then looked up at Vi and Orion. "Thank you for being here. I am so sorry." Once again I couldn't contain my tears as they drifted down my cheeks.

"Stop," Vi said. "I am so glad you send me those emails and texts. It was smart. Guard doesn't want us talking about this until you are well. SO we are dropping this right now. I want to hug you but you are fragile and I certainly don't want to disturb the first sleep Guard has had in two days."

Orion, who had been silent up to this point, finally let it out. "It was the stupidest and bravest thing you did for us, Ava. Shit! I thought Guard was going to fuckin' kill when we figured it all out. He was out of his mind with worry."

"We are going to grab some coffee and we'll be back. I will bring back some food for the both of you. He hasn't eaten either," Vi added.

My eyes slid over to Guard and the warmth of his arm lulled me to close my eyes and drift back off to sleep too.

I woke to Guard stroking my arm and nuzzling my neck.

"Mmm, I love you, Gabriel," I whispered. I heard no response but I felt him kiss my neck.

Nurse Ella returned to find Guard in my bed and gave us forced look of disapproval. It was obvious that it is a half-hearted gesture and a slight smile came across her lips. "Dr. Marrick will be in shortly to check you out Ava. I suggest he only finds one of you in the bed," she teased.

Dr. Marrick was an older man in his late fifties with a very jovial bedside manner. He checked my out fairly quickly and answered all the questions that Guard had. He went so far as to ask about the best way to bathe me. I turned a bright shade of pink and I am sure my mouth hung open for a good thirty seconds and the two men in front of me were talking. I guess I should consider myself fortunate that he didn't ask about when we could have sex.

"Ava, I am going to sign the release papers provided that you have someone with you. I expect your recovering to transform into a normal routine should take several weeks. I do not want you lifting, cleaning, or any other strenuous activity. I do want you to take short walks to get your body moving however with your ankle that will be another week before that is possible." He looked like a dad with his finger pointing at me and continued with, "Do you agree?"

I looked over to Guard and saw his no nonsense clenched jaw and said, "Yes, sir." Not going to argue with either of them with that look of determination on their faces.

"Vi is bringing some clothes. She should be here anytime and I will help you get dressed."

"Okay," I said quietly.

Vi and Orion arrived shortly after our talk with Dr. Marrick. While Guard and Orion were having a chat out in the hall I was able to wriggle my ass into a pair of panties. I had my wide leg yoga pants up to my thighs and was using my one good hand to pull them up little by little. With a final umph, I managed to pull them up and in doing so strained my ribs and shoulder.

I painful groan I could not stop wafted through the room and I find three concerned faces all staring at me once. I able to control my breathing again and the pain subsided.

"Have you lost your mind? What do I have to do to get you to sit still?"

Guard's angry eyes and boring right at me. That was it. I was done. All the fear, sadness, anxiety came leaping forward as I remember the anger that come from Wire and the memories of that night came rushing back like a tidal wave. I burst into uncontrollable tears. One arm held my ribs as the sobs were wrenching through me and was causing my ribs to contract in agony the other covering my face in a useless effort to hide my distress.

"Fuck!" I heard from the doorway.

"Jesus, Guard. Calm the fuck down," Orion, our silent man normally burst forth.

Arms are wrapping around me. "Angel, I'm sorry. I'm a dick." I continue to cry but lean my head on his shoulder. "Baby, I am just so worried. I just can't stand to see you in anymore pain."

I hiccup through my tears to get some semblance of control over myself. I breathe out, "He hit me over and over." I kept going, clinging to Guard's waist. "The knife was cutting into me, I could feel the blood. He was going to touch me." I sobbed in his shirt and finally my tears calmed as he stroked my hair and back.

"Angel, look at me," Guard said quietly. I raised my eyes to his. "He will never, ever bother you again." His voice was steady, firm and determined. "I promise you, baby, he is done." His stone face softened even more, "I am so sorry I scared you. I just can't bear to have anything else happen to you."

"I did this to you," I whispered.

"No, angel. I know you wanted to protect us and we will talk about it when you are better. Right now let me get you home in our bed where I can hold you all night." He smiled at me and I melted into his arms.

"Okay," I sighed wiping the tears away from my eyes.

"Vi, can you help Ava? Orion, bring the car around. I need to make a couple of calls and will be just outside angel."

Vi tenderly works around my shoulder injury and puts me into a wide-sleeved top. We decided against the bra as it was getting to difficult to work around. I was lifted into the car and was quickly tucked in next to Guard as soon as he entered the car.

"Is Becca and Brian still around?" I asked.

"They are at the house making us dinner and looking after Avery. They are waiting for you at home, baby."

"How are you doing back there, Ava?" asks Vi.

"I'm good. It's nice to be around people. I want to sit out on the patio when I get home and enjoy my lake." I look at Guard. "Will you sit with me?"

"Yeah, baby. Of course," he replies and snuggles me closer.

We hit home and Guard refuses to let me walk. I am in his arms and being carried towards to front door and I see Becca bouncing around. "They're here."

We walk through the house to the back towards our patio. "Baby, looks who's here!" Guard exclaimed.

As I turn to see, I hear a whole lot of hooting and howling and I see a sea of Satan's Pride members and their families, just like when we have our barbeques. Guard places me in a lounge chair and adjusts me so that I have pillows and blankets all around. One by one each member came to wish me well. Now my favourite was War and Demon.

War came down on one knee making eye level with me and said, "We will always protect you."

Now Demon who has only ever used five words in my presence dropped to me and quietly said, "You are our Satan's Pride Queen."

More importantly his eyes warmed and for the first time since I met him I see calm and no despair.

I am home and my Satan's Pride men will always protect me because they know I tried to protect them. I know that through this barbeque I napped, ate, smiled and even laughed. Guard stayed by my side and held my hand through it all.

It was later that night when Guard carried me up to bed. Becca helped me undress and brought baby Avery to me and had him snuggle next to me so I could read him a story. He gurgled and laughed making me laugh alongside of him. Becca and I chatted about motherhood and life in New York. We made a pact to visit every couple of months and do a girly day.

The bedroom door swung open and I found Brian hovering over me. He sits on the edge of my bed and takes my hand. "Turtle, we have been through everything together and I never want to go through this one again. I would have been here sooner but I had Becca and Avery in the car; I couldn't drive faster. I could barely talk and I just wanted to get here. Tell me what happened. Please explain to me why you would put yourself in danger like that."

I spent the next while explaining what happened. "I love him, Brian. The idea of losing him when he gave me a part of me I thought was gone forever scared me."

"You love him, huh? Well, I kinda figured that out." He was teasing me. "You ever need me for anything you call me." He kissed my head and sauntered out.

I leaned back into the pillows and closed my eyes. I must have drifted off because when I woke I find myself in Guard's arms. He was awake and I noticed his eyes were moist. Was he crying?

"Angel, I know you did this to protect me and my men but you are never allowed to put yourself in club business again. I should let you go and keep you away from the danger but I can't. I can't live without you. I need you in my life. You make me laugh harder than I ever have. You challenge me, tempt me and make me wild for you. No one makes me lose control like you." He didn't stop there. He kissed my mouth cautiously, not wanting to hurt my bruised lips.

"Thank God you had the foresight to email Vi pictures of the note. Smart of you to send a copy to Milly she ran over within minutes. We headed out there and Orion made some calls to the other MC's to find out what the fuck was going on. We heard that he was causing tension in other clubs too and when they found out they had my woman, they sent their muscle to meet us." He looks shaken and his voice wavers as he says, "I wish I made it there earlier. I wasn't there to protect you. When I saw what he had done I lost my mind. I just beat on him and beat on him. I saw what he did to you and I can't get that picture of you tied to a chair and unconscious on the floor. I will never get that picture out of my head." His voice broke. "I love you, angel. I can't let you go. I promise you that I will do everything in my power to keep you safe."

"Honey, I knew you would find me. I knew you would save me. I just wasn't sure you would want me after making the decision to go." I assured Guard that I made the mistake in not telling him.

"I need you to know something."

"What, baby?"

"I came here to find happiness. I thought that I could dance and teach and live a quiet life filled with peace. Then I found you. You are my happy. I don't want to live without you."

# Chapter 18
# The Wedding Night

Three months later in a villa by the ocean in Maui, Guard and I escaped from the wedding reception. I stand on our balcony looking out at the bonfire on the beach and the tide moving into the beach. The moon is bright and full and the stars are magical lights surrounding us.

Earlier that day I walked down the aisle to marry my wonderful Gabriel "Guard" Stone. I waited patiently as Vi made her way down the aisle followed by Becca. I didn't care what they chose as dresses but they both decided on flowing lilac summer dresses. Each have a slightly different design but they were both beautiful. Orion and Brian waited at the gazebo alter with little Avery serving as our precious ring boy. We wanted our wedding to be fun and comfortable so they wore light coloured pants and white cotton shirts, which were light and airy to combat the heat.

I was holding my purple and pink orchid bouquet and as I looked down the aisle I see my ruggedly handsome badass biker husband to be. He had on black pants and white shirt. I could see his eyes glistening as I neared him. I loved my dress. It is cream coloured lace that hugged my curves and reached my knees. The sleeveless dress showed off my tan and I decided to wear my hair up with soft curls framing my face. I remember the appreciation in Guard's face as I approach.

He took my hand and together we united with our dearest and closed MC family and my best friends.

Guard walks to the balcony with and without saying a word, tugs at my hand and leads me back inside where I find rose petals strewn over our king-size bed. Candles lit the room completely the romantic ambiance.

"I have been waiting patiently for this moment, angel." Guard spoke as his nose edged down mine and followed a path to my neck and kissed and nipped softly until he got to that special spot making me moan softly.

"Can you wait just five more minutes, honey? I have a special surprise for you," I asked sweetly as I unbutton his shirt and trail kisses over his shoulders and slide the shirt off his body.

"Five minutes, baby. I am running out of self-control." He pulls my hips against his and I can feel his hard erection against my abdomen. I slide away begrudgingly but I want to wow him. I slid my hand over him as I grabbed my bag and went into our bathroom.

Guard is on our bed as I step forward so that he can see me. His smile grows wider as I come closer to him. His eyes darken as I climb over to straddle him. I am wearing black boy-cut leather panties and black leather bra. The topper is the motorcycle boots with silver clasps.

"Do you like my biker babe look, honey?" I asked sweetly. I slid my hands into his hair and tugged on it making him look at my face and lick his lips.

"Oh, yeah. Baby, you looking abso-fucking-mazing." His mouth met mine and I was so hot for my sexy biker.

"Gonna go slow, baby. Want this to last," he groaned against my mouth.

His hands roamed my body. The straps of my bra were slid off my shoulders and his tongue traced the path that he was uncovering. After unhooking my bra and tossing it aside I feel his breath hover over my breasts. He licks and blows on each nipple creating a shudder to pierce through my body. He latches onto my right nipple and sucks hard as his hands pulls and rolls the other nipple. I throw my head back giving him more access. I hold his head to my breasts; holding on for more. He pays homage to the other nipple. I am so wet for him and I don't think I can handle anymore.

"Please," I beg.

"I need more, baby."

Guard rolls me over onto my back and I moan in protest and he moves away. His mouth moves down my belly, over to one hip and tracing a path to the other. My hips jerk in an effort to move closer. Guard's hand moves to my ass and gives me a light slap.

116

"Baby, stay still."

"Ah, I can't wait. Please."

"Hush, baby. We're doing this my way."

His fingers hook into the top of my panties and his lowers them inch by inch, kissing my body as he moves them lower and lower. I feel them run down my legs and the warms of his mouth in wet kisses following. He moves them over my boots and off.

"Oh, God."

"You like that? Keeping the boots on. I want to feel them against my back as I fuck you."

"Yes."

"Spread your legs for me, angel."

I quickly comply. My breathing is heavy. My breasts heaving and my hands moving down my stomach.

"Touch yourself, baby. Just like I taught you." I want to please him so I move my fingers tentatively over my clit in a circular motion. I can feel myself getting wetter. Then I feel his hand move mine and hold them in his grasp as he replaces it with his tongue. He licks and takes little nip making me pant and raise my hips for more against his mouth.

"Do you love me, baby?"

"Yes."

"Who do you belong to?"

"You." My voice is straining and I am grinding against his mouth. He takes me to the edge and then relents.

"Please." I can't take much more. "I need you."

"My name, baby. Who do you belong to?"

"You, Gabriel. Just you. Forever you."

He raised himself up and grabs my hips. He lifts them to meet his cock and holds it at the entrance of my pussy. He slams into me hard. I cry out his name and he continues to pound into me. Sliding in and out, gyrating his hips in this methodical movement that make his piercing hit my clit over and over.

I wrap my legs around his back and dig my heels in while my arms pull him close and I bite into his shoulder. I come hard and call for him. That's when I hear his grunts and moans of release as he buries his head in my neck.

Our foreheads meet.

"It just gets better and better, baby," Guard whispers.

# Epilogue

E leven months later and we are planning our anniversary bash. We decided to make this a concert event with neighbouring motorcycle clubs and to show our respect for the truce between us. In total there will be over two hundred. We are making this a family friendly event and later at night we can let loose.

"Honey, I would love to have the 'Smoking Guns' perform," Ava said.

"I asked, angel, and they are happy to do it but they are having trouble getting their female lead to agree."

"But, that's why I want them," Ava replied. "She is so amazing and her voice is beautiful. She rocks hard and she is soulful. I really want her."

"Okay, baby. I will make it happen." Guard is very accommodating. Since he found out Ava was expecting their first little mini-biker, Ava is being doted on.

"I don't want to cause a problem, honey." Ava was serious about this. "I understand that she may have other obligations. It's just that I have all her recordings and Maddie is the most impressive voice I have ever heard."

Guard takes his phone and moves from the patio. "Gonna make it so, baby."

Guard moves to the kitchen while hitting the digits on his voice.

"Yeah, War?"

"Yeah."

"Gotta get Maddie with the Smoking Guns."

"I tried, man. I would do anything for Ava but her brother the lead guitarist said she wasn't available. Fuck!" War was frustrated. He had approached Paul Donelly three times about this and still can't get his sister to agree.

119

"My wife is pregnant and moody. This is our anniversary and this is all she wants. Gotta make this happen. Offer more money. Find a way, friendly, though."

"I tried everything friendly. Her brother says she is actually really shy and she only does a few concerts a year. She shies away from the fame part. She just wants to make music. Fucked if I know what this shit means." War was fed up with this shit. War is used to getting what he wants and not negotiating.

"Take a meeting with Paul. I'll come too. Make it tomorrow afternoon." Guard's wife will not be disappointed.

In the music studio, Paul is laying down a track with the rest of the Smoking Guns, including Maddie. War and Guard make their way to Paul.

"Hey, guys," Paul says.

"Hey." Guard nods, and then continues with "Look, I hear you can't convince Maddie to come out. This is not acceptable. My wife deserves the best and I am going to give her the best." Guard lays it out plain and blunt.

"Look. I have tried to talk reason with Maddie. I don't know what else I can do." Paul looks pretty pissed too. "You think we don't want your money or this gig? We do. Maddie doesn't. The rest of the guys are ready to kill her and I am at my wits end." He runs his hand through his hair. "My sister wants to makes music here in the studio and she will do videos where it is a controlled situation. Concerts is an act for her and she hates them."

"Let me talk to her," Guard states.

"You would scare the hell out of her. Maddie is skittish. Shit happened at a concert a couple of years back and from that moment on she doesn't feel safe. She finds out this is a bunch of biker loaded with beer and vetoed the whole thing. We promised her she would never be alone. We told her that she could leave immediately afterwards. I don't know what else to do." Paul throws his hands in the air in frustration.

"Where is she?" War asks.

"In there recording," and he points to the studio. "Look, she is vulnerable. She is soft and quiet. Definitely not the rocker chick everyone expects." Paul leads them to the studio. "In this spot she doesn't see you." He points to a place in the room where Guard and War move to.

Paul hits the microphone that connects to the recording room. "Maddie, can you do the last verse again for me? I wanna check the sound."

Guard

Maddie turns around. She is unassumingly beautiful. She is long auburn hair with natural curls that reach her lower back. Her eyes are huge and brilliant blue. Her perfect full lips made for kissing and unknowingly brings attention to them by biting her lower lip. She is only five foot four inches tall and definitely has a woman's body with full breasts and proportional hips. Wearing simple boy-cut jeans and loose fitting black top with capped sleeves she approaches the microphone. She is tiny compared to the backup singers.

"Ready," she said quietly.

"On three." Paul holds up his hand and makes the motion of 1-2-3.

The smooth, sexy, soulful voice emerges from such a tiny woman hitting both Guard and War, spiking them to attention.

> Midnight warrior you're what I need.
> Fire feeds your existence.
> Lead me on, oh, baby, lead me there.

Paul turns the volume control to mute and turns to the two men waiting near the door. He looks at them staring at Maddie and the heartfelt delivery of her music.

"Maddie, it's good. Take a break, I'll be just a minute."

Paul walks back out the door followed by Guard and War.

"That's Maddie," he simply said with his hands outstretched. "Not what you expect, right?"

"Fuck. No wonder Ava wants her," War replied.

"Bring her out here," Guard says.

"Won't work. I tell you, I have tried everything."

"Bring. Her. Out. Here," Guard repeats, losing his patience.

"Fine." Paul sighs and moves to the main door.

War looks at Guard and says, "Holy fuck! She is unbelievably hot."

"Glad you think so." Guard laughs.

"What? Why?" War looks concerned at those words.

Maddie walks out with Paul and stops dead at the sight of War and Guard. Her mouth is slightly open and she turns her attention to Paul then back to War and Guard.

"A pleasure to meet you, Maddie." Guard extends his hand. Maddie looks at his hand, then back at her brother and finally puts her hand in his. His hand is twice the size of hers. She shyly lifts her eyes to Guard's and it is noticeable the sigh of relief when Guard let's go.

"Maddie, it seems we have a little problem. My gorgeous pregnant wife wants you to sing at our anniversary concert. I hear that this is issue for you. Lay down the problems and let's see if we can come up with some answers." Guard lays it out, just like that.

"Um…." She looks from Guard to War and back to Guard again. "I don't do many concerts." She starts to back up.

"Tell me why," Guard persists.

"I prefer to record only." Her voice is soft and sweet; musical just like her.

"You're not telling me why," Guard says firmly.

"I don't think that this would be a good idea," she replies again quietly. "I am better in the studio and leave the show to Paul and the guys. He is better at it."

"No offense to your brother but my wife wants you." Guard tries again, "Tell me why?"

Maddie's eyes flit from Guard to War and then she lowers turns to her brother. "I don't want to do this."

Paul pleads, "I swear to you, Maddie, you will never be left unattended. The same shit will never happen to you again."

Maddie crosses her hands in front of her almost shield. "You can't make those promises." Her voice was almost a whisper and she was visibly upset.

"I can guarantee your safety," Guard stated. "I can also guarantee more money."

"It's not about the money," she said quickly.

"What if I give you your own personal bodyguard from the time you drive into the parking lot and I will have him take you home? He will make damn sure that no one comes within five feet of you." Guard is very persistent. "My wife is pregnant and I want her to be happy. You can understand that, can't you, Maddie?"

Maddie is wringing her hands together. "I do understand and I think it's great that you want to make your wife happy, I'm just not sure about this." Her eyes held a tremendous amount of concern.

"I will have my most fierce man by your side until you get home. My word, you'll be safe."

Paul piped up. "Maddie, he swears you'll be safe. Think about what this does for the group." He turns his head to Guard. "Guard will give you his best."

# Guard

"You are looking at my best." Guard motioned to War.

Maddie's face turns to the six-foot-three-inch War, which she had been avoiding eye contact with up until this moment. War looked down on her as well.

"You doubt he can guard you?" asked Guard.

"Um...no. I guess not," Maddie replied hesitantly.

"Any problem taking this on, War?" Guard faced War looking for the answer he already knew he was going to get.

"No," War simply said, still staring at a very agitated Maddie.

"Okay, we are done here. I am going to make my wife's day." Guard looks at Maddie and charmed her with, "Thank you for making me a hero to my wife."

"Looking forward to guarding you, kitten," War utters as Guard turns away.

CPSIA information can be obtained at www.ICGtesting.com
Printed in the USA
LVOW10s1523200916

505435LV00017B/1275/P